FIRE RIVER

Joel   ane is returning to the Circle K
Rar   in New Mexico, the home he left at
fift   . when his mother died. Ten years
lat   e's answering a plea for help from his
fai   that reached him in faraway
W   ing. From a distant ridge, Joel can see
hi   ed father being mistreated by gunmen
w   ave occupied the ranch. Soon he, too,
i   the clutches of Cass Berryman, to
'   l his father has misguidedly willed the
. Against all odds, and with little hope
p, Joel is determined to fight for his
· and his home.

FIRE RIVER

by

Ray Hogan

The Golden West Large Print Books
Long Preston, North Yorkshire,
BD23 4ND, England.

British Library Cataloguing in Publication Data.

MAGNA   7-7-13

Hogan, Ray
     Fire river.

£15-99

A catalogue record of this book is
available from the British Library

ISBN   978-1-84262-933-8 pbk

Published in Large Print 2013 by arrangement with
Golden West Literary Agency

The Golden West Large Print is an imprint of Library Magna
Books Ltd.

Printed and bound in Great Britain by
T.J. (International) Ltd., Cornwall, PL28 8RW

I

Joel Kane looked down from the ridge and studied the small scatter of structures that made up the Circle K. He had realized something was wrong at his father's ranch when he received the letter – and now, having his view of the place, the assumption became a visible fact. Everything was in an advanced state of disrepair: roofs sagged, doors hung from broken hinges, corral poles were down, several missing entirely. Dry leaves, trash, and brush littered the yard. The cottonwood trees that once had spread their thick, protective shade over it all were dead or dying.

Joel considered the scene soberly. It had been ten years since he'd turned his back on the Circle K, vowing never to return, but even in that length of time he knew Amos Kane would not change enough to permit that sort of neglect. Such, actually, had been the seat of their trouble. Amos was a strict, unbending man who demanded perfection in all things. He brooked no excuses, countenanced no variations, insisting that his way alone was the right way. Joel had lived in his despotic shadow until he was fifteen years of age, and then moved on. It was no grievous loss for either. He and Amos had never been close, even after the death of his mother, which ordinarily would have welded the relationship between a father and a son into a firm bond. To the contrary, the chasm between them had widened, just as the bitterness had grown, and thus it was inevitable that the day should come when the boy could stand it no longer.

Consequently, the letter Joel received had come as a shock. It had trailed him four months before finally overtaking him in the Three Forks country of Montana where he was working for Webb Preston. Typical, the note had been brief and to the point.

Need you. Come home, Son.
Amos Kane

Joel's first thought had been: *The old man's hard nose and smart mouth have finally bought him something he can't handle.* Joel had had an impulse to throw the letter away, forget it, but somehow the word Son stuck in his mind. He couldn't recall when Amos had ever employed that term of paternal affection to him. And that his father would actually ask for help had also been astonishing. Amos Kane's creed had been to obligate himself to no one, regardless of need. If a situation arose in which he alone could not handle it, the consequences, however painful, were accepted. It was a narrow, Spartan way of life in which he made no friends and discouraged all overtures, but it was how he wanted it, and all those with whom he came in contact thereafter avoided him and went their own course.

Joel had mulled the matter over for a day and a night before coming to a final decision: he would return to the Circle K to see what it was all about. He owed Amos nothing, but still, he was a Kane – and there was something to the old saw that blood ran thicker than water.

Accordingly, he had loaded his saddlebags with his few belongings, had cut south across a corner of Wyoming, had ridden the depth of Colorado where snow still banked the higher peaks, and had come eventually into the beautiful Fire River country of New Mexico. He had camped one night on the banks of the stream, which took its name from the glow imparted by sunlight striking water flowing over red sandstone, and the following day had skirted the rimrocks to the west of the Circle K, reaching the ridge south of the ranch around mid-morning.

Everything looked the same, Joel thought, except the ranch, and that – he drew himself to sudden attention. Two men emerged from the barn and were strolling lazily toward the main house. One, a squat, huskily built man with a black beard and thick mustache, was twirling a pistol in his right hand. The other, slim, narrow-faced, and dark, wore a bright red bandanna around his neck. They were not working cowhands – that was easy to see. Kane watched them move by the corral where four saddled horses dozed in the warming sunlight, cross the yard, and seat themselves on a log bench near the back door of the ranch house. They were discussing something, and several times the squat one laughed. His partner, however, apparently saw no humor in what was being said; not once did the sober, cold lines of his features relax.

What would men of this sort – obviously gunmen – be doing on the Circle K? Joel ran that question through his mind slowly. Amos Kane had no use for their kind, and more than once Joel had watched his father, shotgun cradled in his long arms, order them off the property when they paused, supposedly looking for work. Suspicion began to build slowly within Kane. Men such as those two would not be there unless something – or someone – had forced Amos to permit it.

That fact, coupled with the general run-down appearance of the ranch, could only mean... Again Joel's thoughts came to a stop. The screen door leading off the kitchen at the rear of the house opened, and an old man, water bucket in hand, shuffled out into the yard. He was tall, angular, and bent with years; his hair was iron-gray and shoulder-length. The clothing he wore was faded and torn and hung slackly from his frame.

Head down, the oldster walked haltingly toward the well. The thick-set gunman said something to him. He paused, half turned, and looked to the south. Shock traveled through Joel. There was no mistaking that sharp, hawk-like face. The old man was his father, Amos Kane.

The outlaw with the pistol raised it and leveled it at Amos. The dry clack of the hammer being cocked carried clearly across the hush. Abruptly the gunman laughed, as he lowered his weapon. Amos Kane stared at him briefly and then, shrugging wearily, plodded on toward the well. Joel watched in disbelief. This was not the Amos Kane he knew and remembered; this was an old, broken man, devoid of spirit, and utterly without hope.

The windlass creaked loudly. Amos wound up a dipper keg of water, poured it into his bucket. Grasping the bail, he swung slowly about and started back for the house. When he drew abreast of the toughs, the thin one thrust out a foot, Amos tripped and went to his knees, spilling the water and sending his tormentors into uproarious laughter.

Anger now a steady flame within him, Joel watched his father pull himself stiffly to his feet, retrieve the bucket, and return to the well. Again the windlass squealed its protest, and once more Amos Kane filled his bucket. Cautiously, now, he wheeled and headed for the door, but this time he swung wide to avoid the men on the bench, who continued to laugh and taunt him until he had finally disappeared into the house.

Joel remained motionless, anger and wonder filling him with a harsh grimness.

There was no doubt now that his father was in some sort of desperate trouble, and he no longer questioned the old man's change of heart and his appeal for help. Forgotten were all the differences of the past, all the bitterness. Joel Kane saw only that his father needed him – and, judging from his frail appearance and evident weakness, needed him quickly.

He considered his best move. It would be foolhardy simply to ride down, announce himself, and attempt to drive the outlaws off the ranch. There were more inside the house – at least two, if he could calculate from the number of horses waiting near the corral. There could be more in the barn or elsewhere on the Circle K. He'd play it smart – go down and ask for a job. There would be nothing unusual in that. Cowboys were always on the move, and hardly a day passed when a rancher did not have two or three dropping by, looking for work. In that way he could get a closer look at them, size up the situation, and figure out his next move.

Before he could make any plans at all he must know just what he was up against. There was one drawback in following that course: if Amos recognized him, he would be in immediate trouble unless he could somehow warn the older man in time. He gave that several minutes' thought and then shrugged. It was a risk he'd have to run, he concluded. Heeling his sorrel horse lightly, he started down the long slope.

II

Kane reached the edge of the yard, broke through the fringe of encroaching rabbit-brush and snakeweed, and pulled up beside the four horses standing near the corral. He swung from the saddle with studied, deliberate movements, hearing rather than seeing the two men by the house rise and drift quietly toward him. Taking his time, he looped the sorrel's reins around a pole and turned. The outlaw wearing the red bandanna blocked him on the right; the husky one had taken up a position to the left.

'Now, where do you think you're going, mister?'

The squat rider stood, legs apart, thumbs hooked in his belt.

Joel forced a grin. 'Looking to see the head man.'

The outlaw threw a sardonic glance to his partner. 'You hear that, Clete? He's wanting to see the head man. What do you reckon for?'

The thin-faced gunman's expression did not change. 'Maybe he'll tell us,' he drawled.

Joel could feel the steady press of their eyes upon him, sizing him up, making their assessment. 'Need a job. Figured to try here.'

Clete folded his arms across his chest, spat, and nodded to the husky man. 'Haven't heard of any jobs around here, have you, Bill?'

Kane, too, had been judging quietly. Bill would be a brawler. Clete was the more dangerous of the two – a man who lived by his gun. It was written there in the flat, emotionless depths of his eyes, in the stillness that lay upon him.

'Sure haven't,' Bill said. 'So you might as well mount up, cowboy, and ride on.'

The frozen grin did not leave Joel's lips. 'Reckon I'll let your boss tell me that.'

'Far as you're concerned,' the squat outlaw snapped, 'I'm the boss of this outfit ... and I'm telling you!'

Kane clung to his temper. After seeing their treatment of his father, he would like nothing better than taking on the two men and teaching them a lesson, but he couldn't afford to at that moment. It wasn't in him, however, to back down.

'You look like the hired help to me,' he said, starting for the house.

'The hell... I'll show you!' Bill yelled, and lunged.

Joel took a quick half step to the side. He

reached out, caught the husky rider by one shoulder, and spun him off balance. Placing both hands against Bill's shoulders, Kane shoved him hard into Clete. Both men swore as they came together. Kane, drawing his pistol, glanced to the barn where two more figures, attracted by the shouts, rushed into the open, then halted.

'Damn you... I'll pull you apart!' Bill gritted, regaining his balance and wheeling fast.

Kane nodded and looked beyond him to Clete. The outlaw's hand rested lightly on the butt of his pistol. He made no further move, aware of the weapon already in Joel's grasp. In that same instant Bill charged. Once more Kane pulled away. As the husky rider rushed in, Joel raised his arm and clubbed the man sharply on the side of the head. Bill groaned and went to his knees.

Eyes still on Clete and conscious of the two men now approaching from the barn, Joel turned half around, keeping them all within his field of vision. He bobbed his head coldly at Clete.

'Either draw that thing, or forget it.'

The gunman did not move.

Kane's eyes hardened. 'Maybe you'd better get rid of it,' he said. 'Use your left hand.'

Clete considered for a long moment, then, reaching across, drew his pistol and tossed it into the brush.

Joel brought his attention back to Bill. The bearded outlaw was on his knees, shaking his head to clear away the cobwebs. Over to his left the pair from the barn had halted and were watching narrowly. Neither was armed. Hostlers, Joel guessed, hired to look after the horses and gear. He dismissed them from his mind.

Sliding his weapon back into its holster, he reached down, grasped Bill by the arm, and dragged him upright. 'You done?'

Bill jerked free. 'Hell no, I ain't done!' he shouted, and struck out savagely.

The unexpected blow caught Kane in the ribs, sending a stab of pain through his body. He grinned at his own carelessness and danced away to avoid the man's lumbering rush.

'Get him, Bill,' Clete said in a taut, hopeful voice. 'Back him up against the corral.'

Kane halted abruptly, struck out with a straight left, followed by a swinging right. The left stalled the outlaw in his tracks; the right rocked him to his heels. Clete said something else, but the words were lost to Kane. The hostlers had eased in nearer, and he realized he was pressing his luck – if they all moved in at once. He smashed another right into Bill's middle, drove a second blow straight into the outlaw's jaw. Bill began to wilt. Relentless now, Kane moved in close, chopped the husky rider with a vicious right, cocked his left for a finishing follow-up, then hesitated. Bill was sinking slowly. Stepping back quickly, Joel dropped his hand to his pistol. The hostlers checked themselves. Clete, absolutely motionless, watched in silence.

Joel met Clete's gaze, and then shifted his hot glance to the hostlers. Both looked down. At that moment a voice from the house cut through the sudden quiet.

'What's going on out there?'

Kane turned. A tall, powerfully built man with flaming red hair had come into the open. Behind him, a Mexican in *vaquero* trappings lounged in the doorway of the house.

'You're getting what you wanted,' Clete said.

Joel continued to stare at the redhead. 'Who's he?'

'Berryman ... Cass Berryman.'

The name struck no familiar chord in Kane's mind. 'He the foreman?'

'He's the whole damned works,' Clete said dryly. 'You were looking for...'

'Clete!' Berryman shouted again. 'What's the trouble down there?'

The thin-faced gunman wheeled lazily. 'Jasper here rode in looking for you. Wants a job. Bill got some other ideas.'

Berryman considered that. 'Ideas about what?'

'About hiring, I reckon.'

'Bill's getting a mite too big for his britches,' the red-haired man said angrily. 'Bring him on up here.'

He turned, started for the door, paused, and waved at the two hostlers. 'One of you throw a bucket of water on Taney, get him to his feet,' he said, and pushed by the *vaquero* into the house.

Both men hurried toward the water trough. Clete eyed Kane and jerked his head.

'You heard him. Get moving.'

Joel Kane nodded, took a forward step, and then pulled to a halt as Clete veered aside to retrieve his pistol. The outlaw caught Kane's steady attention on him and shrugged. 'No sweat,' he murmured, and dropped the weapon into its holster.

Joel shrugged. 'Just for luck, I'll walk behind.'

The gunman made no answer, but simply strode on, his booted feet sending up small geysers of dust each time they touched the ground. It must have been a dry winter, Kane thought absently. Back near the corral there was a sudden splash of water followed by a mumbled curse. The hostlers had brought the black-bearded Bill Taney to consciousness.

Reaching the house, Clete leaned forward and pulled open the dust-clogged screen door. Joel paused and shook his head. The outlaw's eyes flickered, but he moved on, and Kane trailed him into the room. Halting, the younger man glanced around, at once remembering old and familiar objects from the days gone. He was in the kitchen. The big nickel-trimmed Pacific cook stove still stood in the corner; the heavy, oblong table his father had built, along with the two benches that served as chairs, were still in use. On the wall was the framed lithograph depicting a platter heaped with apples and peaches, still in its exact place – nothing had changed.

'What kind of work're you looking for?'

Cass Berryman's voice had a deep harshness to it. Joel brought his wandering attention to a halt. The red-haired man stood near the door that led into the rest of the house. At his elbow was the sly-faced Mexican. Across the room a turkey-necked, balding oldster with a stringy mustache worked over a narrow bench built against the wall. He was peeling potatoes and slicing them into an iron spider. Amos Kane was not in evidence. Joel breathed a bit deeper as he realized that.

'Cows,' he said. 'Been working cattle all my life.'

'Not all you've been doing,' Berryman said, glancing through the doorway to the corral. 'Somebody tell you I was taking on hands?'

Joel shook his head. 'Saw your place. Looked pretty big, so I figured it'd be a good bet to stop.'

Berryman considered that. He glanced at the *vaquero,* then at Clete. 'Where'd you come from?' he asked, bringing his eyes back to Kane.

'North ... several places.'

The Circle K was no longer a working ranch, that much Joel had already decided. Just what did go on under the guise of cattle raising he had yet to learn – just as he needed to know where Cass Berryman and his hardcases fit.

'You come through town?'

'Town?' Joel repeated, making a question of it. The less they thought he knew of the country, the better.

'Cedar River. Twenty miles east or so of us.'

Kane shook his head. 'Wasn't anything but open country, the way I rode in.' He looked up as the doorway filled and Bill Taney stepped into the room. The bearded man's face was beginning to swell, and there was a dark welt under one eye. Berryman gave him critical appraisal.

'Never learn, do you?'

Taney's features reddened, and he took a step forward. 'I'm not done with that god-damn' saddle bum yet! I aim to...'

Berryman waved him back. 'Like I said, you never learn.'

'Took me when I wasn't looking,' Bill grumbled, glancing at Clete. The gunman only stared.

Berryman came back to Joel. 'Nothing

much doing around here as far as cattle goes. Handle a few head now and then. More interested in a man who can use his fists ... and his gun.'

'Done my share of that kind of work, too. Not backing off, but just what'll I be doing?'

'Special sort of jobs ... for me.'

'Jobs like robbing a bank, maybe?'

Berryman laughed, a hollow, mirthless sort of sound. 'Could be. We keep plenty busy around here,' he said, and pulled aside slightly.

Amos Kane, moving unsteadily, came through the doorway. At close range he appeared even worse off than he had from the ridge. There was a starved look to his sunken, lined face, and his eyes had receded into deep, shadowy pockets. One corner of his mouth sagged noticeably, and the firm set of his jaw that Joel always remembered was gone.

'Hurry it up, old man,' Cass Berryman snapped impatiently.

Amos stumbled slightly in his haste,

caught himself against the table. He looked up at Joel. A frown pulled at his brow, and his lips tightened briefly.

'You hear me?' Berryman snarled and, reaching out, gave the oldster a hard shove.

Anger whipped through Joel. He drew up stiffly, thrust out an arm to steady Amos. The old man nodded, pulled free, and crossed over to where the cook still worked at his counter.

'Well, what about it?'

Berryman's voice cut into Joel Kane's suppressed fury. Lowering his head to hide the tautness of his features, he shrugged. 'Not sure I want that kind of work.'

'Why not? Be no chore to you ... especially when word gets out how you cleaned Bill's plow.'

'It's not getting around,' Taney broke in hotly, ''cause I figure to change things first.'

'You haven't done much good so far,' Berryman taunted.

'We'll see about that,' Bill yelled, and lunged at Joel.

Amos Kane, in the process of crossing to the stove, moved into the outlaw's path. The two men collided. Taney swore, struck out wildly. The blow drove Amos to his knees. Taney kicked him savagely in the ribs. The old man groaned, fell forward.

Blinding fury rocked Joel. Forgetting his precautions, he stepped in fast, smashed a hard blow to Bill Taney's belly. As the outlaw buckled, he straightened him up with a stiff uppercut. Taney staggered back, hands clutching his middle, mouth blared wide as he gasped for wind. Joel, thoroughly aroused, closed in swiftly. He heard Berryman yell something, and then caught a fleeting glimpse of the *vaquero* coming at him from the left. He jerked away, came up solidly against Clete. Spinning, he rapped the gunman with a short left, started a right.

'Joel ... look out!'

His father's frantic warning caused him to duck, wheel again. He had a quick vision of the Mexican swinging his pistol at his head, pulled back. The blow missed, and the Mexican, off balance, reeled by. Joel gave the man a hard shove, sending him crashing into the wall, and wheeled once again to face Clete.

'Hold it!'

Cass Berryman's harsh voice overrode the confusion. Joel, barely hearing, swung wild at Clete, missed. Momentum carried him into the outlaw, and for a moment they were locked together. A gunshot blasted inside the room with deafening effect. Joel felt Clete's arms loosen as Berryman's voice again sounded.

'You hear me? Stand away, all of you! I'll shoot the next man who tries anything!'

Joel, arms at his sides, turned slowly. Clete had pulled him back against the wall and was breathing heavily. Bill Taney still held his belly, and the Mexican, a knife in his hand, was crouched in a corner.

Berryman, holstering his revolver, gave Joel a quick glance, and then stepped to where Amos was struggling to regain his feet. Leaning down, he grasped the older man by the arm and pulled him upright.

'Did I hear you right?' he demanded, shaking Amos roughly. 'You called him Joel?'

The elder Kane said nothing.

Light flared in Cass Berryman's eyes. Raising his hand, he slapped Amos across the face sharply. 'Answer me damn you!'

The old man's head wobbled grotesquely. Joel surged forward, fresh anger overcoming him. Abruptly he halted, feeling the hard, round pressure of Clete's pistol against his spine.

'Leave him alone,' he said, facing Berryman. 'Sure, he called me Joel ... it's my name.'

III

A slow smile parted Cass Berryman's lips, and a slyness came into his eyes. He leaned back against the table.

'Well, what do you know,' he said in a

quiet, satisfied way. 'The old he-bear's cub has come home.'

The *vaquero* looked up, frowned. 'This is the son?'

'This is the son,' Berryman said. 'The old man used to talk about him a few years back. Haven't heard much about him lately, and I reckon he just sort of slipped my mind.'

From across the room Bill Taney, finally recovered, said: 'That change things any?'

Berryman shook his head and stared at Joel. 'What brought you back? The old man send for you?'

'Just riding by,' the younger Kane said.

Berryman wagged his head slowly, the frozen grin still breaking his lips. 'That's a god-damn' lie. You wouldn't have come in here asking for a job, if that was it.'

'Suit yourself,' Joel answered disinterestedly. He glanced at Amos, and temper stirred him again, but he held himself in check. He'd stand no chance bucking the four of them. It'd be best to bide his time, try to figure a way out without a showdown.

'I'm asking you ... what do you want?'
Cass Berryman's voice had dropped to a
lower pitch.

'I have to want something?' Joel countered.
'Can't a man drop by to see his folks?'

The red-haired outlaw chief shook his
head again. 'Amos told me you'd up and run
off. You wouldn't be coming back now
unless you had a reason.'

Berryman was prying, digging, trying to
learn what he knew, Joel realized. So far that
totaled up to nothing except that his father
apparently was a helpless prisoner on his
own ranch.

'You heard my reason. Just dropped by.'

'Hogwash!' Berryman snapped, and then
leaned forward. 'Who'd you talk to in Cedar
River?'

'Never came that way. Do I have to say
everything twice for you?'

Bill Taney muttered a curse and shifted
restlessly on his feet. Berryman motioned to
Clete.

'Take his iron,' he ordered, and then to

Joel added: 'I figure you're lying.'

The gunman pressed up close to Joel, lifted the Forty-Five from its holster, thrust it under his own belt. Immediately Cass Berryman lashed out and struck the younger Kane across the mouth.

'I want some straight talk ... you hear?'

Fighting anger, Joel brushed at the blood oozing from his crushed lips. 'You heard it right. I've talked to nobody.'

Berryman stared at the younger man intently for a long minute. Finally he shrugged. 'Maybe it is the truth,' he said with a sigh.

Bill Taney pushed forward instantly. 'Let me have him, Cass,' he begged. 'I'll sure as hell get it out of him.'

'Doubt that. You haven't looked so good mixing in with him so far. Anyway, he's not the talking kind.'

'I got ways,' the husky outlaw promised.

Berryman only smiled, turned lazily to Amos. 'How about you, old man? You want to do some talking?'

Amos Kane, head bowed, stood motion-less. Cass, suddenly angered, grasped him by the shirt front, jerked him up sharply. 'You send for your pup? You tell him how things are around here?'

Amos turned away. Berryman yanked again, almost pulling the older man off his feet. Instantly Joel pushed in between the two and knocked the outlaw's arm aside.

'Let him be,' he said coldly, ignoring the gun Clete held to his back. 'You don't and I'll kill you.'

Berryman's eyes flared with surprise, and then his grin returned. 'Expect you would at that ... leastwise you'd try.'

'Let me take care of him, Cass,' Bill Taney pleaded in that same anxious way.

Berryman shook his head. 'And have him lying around for somebody to find and start asking questions? Not much. I've got a better idea.'

'Ain't no idea better'n getting rid of him before he stirs up trouble,' Taney muttered.

'Not saying there is. I'm talking about the

how of it.'

'The how?'

'Sure. This is something that's got to be done right. Can't have anybody questioning my inheritance.'

A grin spread slowly across Bill Taney's bearded face. The *vaquero* laughed. Amos Kane turned his head and looked at Joel helplessly.

'The way I see it the time's come to collect, especially since we've got the pup here, too. Now I can handle things first-rate, without any loose strings hanging down ... no heirs to worry about.'

Joel could make no sense of Cass Berryman's words. He was wishing now that Berryman didn't know he hadn't been in Cedar River. It seemed to have an important bearing on the situation.

Taney scratched at his beard, cocked his head to one side. 'But how are you going to collect this inheritance thing without...?'

'Without a fuss? Easy.' Berryman glanced around the room. 'We'll just pay a little visit to Mud Lake.'

Mud Lake, Joel remembered, was a swale ten miles or so across the valley that had been a deathtrap for many an unwary steer and horse. Fed by underground springs, the sink was filled with a thin, slimy clay that quickly engulfed any luckless creature blundering onto its surface, much as did the quicksands of the Rio Grande.

'Sure ... that's just the ticket!' Taney yelled. 'The old man and the pup'll just drop out of sight ... and you'll take over.'

'All according to law,' Berryman finished.

Except for the promise of death outlined for him and his father, it was no more than a jumble of words to Joel Kane, but he wasted no time endeavoring to puzzle them out. He knew only that he must act quickly, that, if he delayed longer, he would be in no position to do anything. Whirling, he drove his elbow into Clete's belly, knocked away the pistol the outlaw was jamming against his body. As the gun exploded harmlessly, he leaped for Cass Berryman.

He caught the man by the neck, struggled to spin him around, to use him as a shield while he clawed for the pistol in the other's holster. Berryman yelled, hung onto the edge of the table. The *vaquero* rushed in, knife glittering in his hand. He went down abruptly, tripped by Amos Kane.

Berryman yelled again, began to thrash wildly about. Joel felt his grip slipping, felt other hands pulling at him. He shook loose, tried to leap onto the table and get behind Cass Berryman, but he was being held down. His fingers slipped, and he realized Berryman's throat was in his grasp. He shut down tight, felt the outlaw shudder.

'Call them off!' he shouted. 'Or you're dead!'

A wave of pain slashed at him as Clete, or one of the others, struck him across the back of the head with a gun barrel. He fought off the clouds of darkness that were swirling about him, tightened his grip. Berryman began to wilt. Another blow smashed into his head. As if from a great distance he could hear someone yelling. He could feel himself sinking, falling away. And then it was completely dark.

IV

Joel Kane opened his eyes. It was half dark, hot and stuffy, and it was several minutes before he realized he was lying on the floor in a small, windowless room. He remained motionless, conscious of dull, throbbing pain, while he endeavored to get his bearings. A slight sound caught his attention. Turning only his eyes, he saw the bent silhouette of his father hunkered beside him. Unsteady, he pulled himself to one elbow. Instantly the older man leaned forward.

'You all right, Son?'

Amos Kane's voice was anxious. Joel nodded slowly and, then remembering, said: 'How long have we been in here?'

'Half hour or so.'

'Where are we?'

'Storeroom. Off the end of the house.'

Joel couldn't recall the room, guessed his father must have built it after he had gone.

'Was afraid Jordan had done you in.'

'Jordan?'

'Clete. The one holding a gun on you. Hit you with it a couple of times when you jumped on Berryman.'

Joel's senses were finally clearing despite the unrelenting pain. Touching the back of his head gingerly, he drew himself upright and made a slow tour of the room. There was only the one door around which light filtered to provide meager illumination.

'Joel,' the elder Kane said hesitantly, 'it's good to see you again. But I'm wishing now I hadn't sent that letter. Didn't aim to get you in a fix like this.'

Joel returned to his father's side and sat down. He could feel the stiffness between them, a sort of barrier. 'It's all right, Pa,' he said, trying to brush it away. 'Not the first fight I've been in ... probably not the last. They hurt you?'

'Nope. Reckon I'm used to it.'

Silence hung between them after that for a long minute, and then Joel said: 'Who's this Cass Berryman?'

Amos stirred wearily. 'Biggest mistake I ever made ... and I've made some humdingers, like letting you leave.'

'We both had a hand in that. Don't blame it all on yourself.'

'My fault ... just the same. I did a lot of regretting later.'

Again there was quiet. 'Berryman,' Joel pressed gently. 'What about him?'

'Was my foreman. Been working for me seven, eight years. One of the best ... or was in the beginning.'

'What made him change?'

The old man wagged his head. 'Don't rightly know. Things were running along pretty well. The stock was doing fine, market stayed high, and we were having a stretch of good winters and summers. I sort of started taking it easy. I was getting a mite tired, so I just let Cass handle everything, run things to suit himself.'

'And he finally took over everything.'

'That's what he did. I woke up one day to find all my boys gone, and Cass had new help on the place ... his boys, only they weren't regular cowhands ... they were tough hardcases who didn't know anything about cattle raising.'

'They the only kind around now ... gunfighters?'

'No. Berryman's got half a dozen to take care of the stock he brings in.'

'Brings in?'

Amos Kane lowered his head. 'Rustled stuff. They drive it in, small jags mostly. Then they use running irons, change the brands to Circle K, and sell it off as my stock.'

'And nobody ever catches on?' Joel asked in an amazed voice.

'Reckon nobody even thinks about it. Like I said, Cass and his crowd pick stock up in small bunches, and when there's a sale made

... usually to the Army or one of the Indian agents ... the steers all carry the Circle K brand.'

Joel nodded. 'People just naturally don't figure you'd be mixed up in anything like rustling.'

'That's it. Nobody'd bother to check, anyway.'

Joel could understand that. Amos had closed his gates to any who would be friendly. As a result he was left strictly alone by other ranchers and townspeople.

'Can't you do something about it when a sale is made? There're papers to be signed...?'

'Part of that mistake I was telling you about. Cass handles everything, does all the business for me. I gave him that authority.' The older Kane paused, then said: 'You know, I haven't been off the place in five years.'

'Five years,' Joel echoed. 'He's keeping you prisoner?'

'Just what he's doing. It's been more'n a year since I was farther'n yelling distance of this house.'

'And now he figures to get rid of you ... of both of us ... for good in Mud Lake.' Joel frowned, remembering something else Cass Berryman had mentioned. 'What's this inheritance thing he was talking about?'

Amos Kane sighed deeply, rubbed at his jaw. 'It was the biggest fool thing of all that I did.'

Joel stared at his parent through the gloom. 'He's actually going to inherit the Circle K, when you're dead?'

'That's the way I fixed it. It came up about a year ago. Cass made me a proposition. Mentioned I was getting old. Said if I'd make out a will giving him the ranch when I was gone, he'd take care of me the rest of my days. Deal was, I'd have a roof over my head, grub, spending money, and somebody to look after me when I couldn't get around on my own. Sounded like a fair offer at the time, and I took him up on it. The will was made out, giving him everything, all legal and such. He even brought Henry Testman out from the bank to do the witnessing.'

Impatience stirred through Joel. Amos Kane should have known better, and words to that effect sprang to his lips, but he let them go unsaid. Amos was old, and he was tired. Berryman's offer would have sounded good. He was suddenly aware of his father's intent stare.

'You see,' the older man said, 'the way things were, I never expected to lay eyes on you again.'

'I understand, Pa,' Joel answered quietly. 'What made you send me that letter?'

'I finally woke up to what was happening. Things went along fairly well for a few months, then I could see Cass was changing. He and his bunch started pushing me around, making my life mighty miserable. Didn't take much thinking to realize what was up ... the sooner I was dead, the sooner Cass could take over. That's when I slipped a drifter a gold eagle to mail a letter to you. It was all I could figure left to do.'

'Surprised you knew where to find me.'

42

'There was a pack peddler through here about a year before that. Said he'd run into you up Wyoming way.'

Joel remembered the man. They'd met accidentally in a saloon, got to talking. When the peddler mentioned he was going down into the Fire River country, Joel had told him that was his home, that his father had a ranch near the town of Cedar River.

'Took that letter four months to catch up,' Joel said. 'I'd moved on twice.'

'I was wrong to send it. All it did was bring you back so's you could get yourself killed.'

'Not dead yet,' Joel murmured. 'There anybody we can go to for help?'

'Can't think of anyone. The way Cass does things, it all seems to be on the up and up. Be a mite hard to get anybody to believe what I've told you.'

Such was the truth, Joel realized. Berryman was smart – smart enough to keep his dealings strictly legal – and anything that was to be done he would have to do it. The will seemed to be the key to the situation. As it now stood, the paper was nothing less than a death warrant. If he could get his hands on it, destroy it... 'Who's the bunch Berryman keeps with him?'

'They handle the rough stuff. Bill Taney and Clete Jordan and the Mexican, Dobe Rivera. Those three are always with Cass.'

'How about the cook?'

'Name's Ben Stoyers. Never known him to lean one way or the other. Sort of gets along with everybody.'

'He stand by you or with Berryman?'

Amos considered that. 'Ain't sure. Been with me about ten years, little less. Only old hand left on the place.'

Joel rose to his feet and crossed to the door. Placing his ear to the widest crack, he listened. He could hear nothing. Apparently Berryman and his outlaw hired hands were not inside the house – but there was no way to be sure. There was also the possibility of a guard posted somewhere nearby. He turned back to Amos.

'Got to figure a way out of here. Can't risk

breaking down that door. Any ideas?'

Amos started to move his head negatively, and then sat up straighter. 'Just happened to remember that I ran out of nails when I was putting down this floor. There's a couple of boards over there in that corner that I didn't fasten.'

Joel hurried to the opposite side of the small room, began to pull away several sacks and other odds and ends piled there.

'Always intended to finish the job,' Amos said, moving to his side. 'Just kept forgetting, I guess.'

'Good thing that you did,' Joel replied, dropping to his knees. Thrusting a finger into a knothole, he tried one of the planks. It came up easily. The one next to it was also loose. The third, however, had been anchored securely. It didn't matter.

'Wide enough to crawl through,' Joel said. 'What's it like under the floor?'

Amos thought back. 'Joists're about a foot off the ground.'

'Any openings in the foundation?'

'No foundation. I just piled rocks at each corner and set the timbers on them. Be easy getting out. And there're tall weeds all around. Nobody's apt to spot you until you get into the open.'

'Us,' Joel corrected. 'You're coming with me.'

'No. I'd just be in the way. I got into this mess. It's only right I don't hurt your chance of getting out.'

'We'll get out of it together,' Joel said firmly.

Amos stared at the younger man for a long moment, and then nodded humbly. 'All right, Son. Whatever you say. Only thing ... what do we do once we're free?'

'First thing'll be to get you to a safe hiding place. Then I aim to get back that will you signed. It's Berryman's trump card. Once I've done that, then we'll be holding the aces.'

The elder Kane grinned into the darkness. 'For a fact! Tearing that paper up'll put an end to his game powerfully quick. Getting it, howsoever, is going to be a sizable chore.'

'I know that, but I'll ford that creek when

46

I come to it. Main thing is to get out of here before somebody shows up. You ready?'

'Ready,' Amos said.

Joel lowered himself through the narrow opening in the floor and stretched out full length on the cool earth beneath. There was scarcely room to move, but by keeping himself prone he wormed his way to one side. While he waited for Amos, he glanced around.

Sunlight trickled through the thick brush and weeds growing along the edge of the structure, and he easily determined the location of the corners where Amos had stacked flat rocks to support the timbers. It would be wise to emerge from a side not facing the yard, he decided, and turned his head to see how Amos was faring.

The older man was clear of the opening and now behind him. Joel immediately began to work his way toward the far side. He was anxious to get away from the house as soon as possible. Likely Berryman planned to wait until nightfall before taking them to Mud

Lake, so every minute gained would put them that much further ahead of the outlaws.

He reached the edge of the building and halted. Amos was a few feet away, pulling himself painfully along. It was a hard task for the older man, and his strained features reflected the effort. When he caught up, Joel touched him on the shoulder.

'I'll go first and have a look around. If it's clear, I'll call.'

Amos signified his understanding, and Joel, reaching forward, brushed aside a narrow tunnel in the rank growth and crawled into the open. He lay there a full minute, listening carefully. From the muted sounds coming from the kitchen, he guessed the cook was busy preparing the midday meal. Convinced there was no one close by, Joel finally raised himself to his knees and, turning, threw his glance into the yard. It was deserted – even to the horses that had been standing near the corral.

That was a disappointment. He had planned to make use of them, taking his own sorrel and one of the outlaws' mounts for his father. Now he would have to risk entering the barn. There was one good thing: the absence of the horses meant Berryman and the others were off somewhere and not hanging around the house. He wouldn't need to worry about encountering any of them.

Turning, he leaned down into the opening in the weeds and whispered: 'All clear.' He braced himself to give whatever assistance he could to his father. A few moments later they were crouched in the tall, musty-smelling rabbitbrush at the edge of the yard.

'Need horses ... and a gun,' Joel said, looking toward the barn. 'Are there likely to be more than those two hostlers I saw working when I rode in?'

'Never is,' Amos replied. 'We can get horses, sure enough. Got my doubts about a gun.'

'Rifle on my saddle,' Joel said. 'If they put my sorrel in the barn...'

'That's where he'll be.' Amos pointed to the end of the sprawling building. 'Side door over there. Be easier getting in that way instead of the front.'

Joel nodded, took a quick survey of the surrounding area to assure himself no one was near, and started along the rear of the corrals for the larger structure. They reached the side entrance without incident. There was no concealing brush at that point, and they were in the open, but Joel spent a full minute listening, trying to locate the two men he expected to be inside. He could hear nothing, however, except the occasional movement of a horse. Bending low, he drew back the door carefully. With Amos close on his heels, he moved into the gloomy interior of the structure.

Cautioning the older man, Joel continued down the corridor-like area in front of several empty stalls until he reached the intersecting runway. There he halted abruptly. The two hostlers were just inside the front doors. One sat propped against the wall, dozing. The other was indifferently mending harness.

In the stalls directly across from them Joel could see the heads of several horses. He located his sorrel in the second compartment. Turning back, he rejoined Amos.

Getting the horses was going to be difficult. There was no approach except up the runway, and he had no weapon of any sort. While the hostlers – as he had noted earlier – were unarmed, they could yell, set up an alarm, and bring someone who did possess a weapon.

Joel related this to Amos, who nodded his understanding of the problem. When the younger man had finished, he thought for a moment, and then pointed to a corner on the opposite side of the runway.

'Tools stacked over there. Maybe you just might find something we could use.'

Immediately Joel returned to the intersection, looked again to the hostlers. Both now dozed. Signaling to Amos, he waited for the older man, and together they crossed over and moved to the tool bin. The most powerful weapon appeared to be a pick handle. Joel chose one, turned away, and then paused when he saw Amos also take up one of the lengths of hickory. The oldster grinned.

'Figure I might get a chance to help.'

Joel smiled back, and together they returned to the runway. The hostlers had not stirred. Moving quietly, Joel worked his way along from stall to stall toward them. Amos was no more than a step behind.

They gained the partition occupied by a barrel-bodied little buckskin just below the two men. Joel could see his horse by looking over the intervening cross boards, felt relief when he saw the sorrel was still saddled and bridled, that his rifle was yet in its scabbard. They would need time only to throw gear on a mount for Amos.

He brought his attention back to the hostlers. He would move in silently, knock out the nearest man with a blow on the head, turn quickly, and fell the second man before he could cry out, if possible. If he...

Joel drew back abruptly as a sudden rush of hoofs sounded in the yard. The hostlers came alive and bounded to their feet. Joel swore under his breath. Berryman and the others had returned.

He watched the four outlaws wheel up to the corral and swing down. One of the hostlers sauntered into the open, looking expectantly at Berryman. The outlaw leader turned away and, with the others trailing, walked to the house and entered. The stable-man shrugged, then returned to where his partner waited.

'Reckon they aim to ride out again.'

The older man of the pair grunted. 'Bill said something about being busy tonight ... reason they didn't want the sorrel put in the back. You about done with that harness?'

'Just about.'

'Soon's you are, we'll...' The hostler stopped, stared across the runway. 'Say, who...?'

Joel gathered his muscles, pressed hard against the side of the stall. The man had spotted him.

'What's wrong?'

'Thought I saw somebody ... in there with

the buckskin.'

The younger man laughed. 'What's eating you, Ike? You going loco? Nobody but us has come in here since morning.'

'Just the same, I think I saw something,' Ike insisted and moved toward the stall.

Kane waited, muscles tense. The hostler reached the corner of the partition and stepped in closer. Silent as a shadow, Joel brought the pick handle down in a short, swift arc. Ike grunted, dropped to the straw-littered floor.

'Find anything?' the younger man called.

'Only me,' Joel said, leaping from the depths of the stall and swinging the pick handle in a single motion.

The hostler slammed back against the wall, doubled forward, and sprawled in the runway. Joel tossed the length of hickory aside and, taking the man by the shoulders, dragged him out of sight. Amos, wasting no time, was already busy throwing gear on a long-legged gray in the adjoining stall.

Chore completed, Joel backed the sorrel

into the runway. While he waited for Amos, he checked the rifle. It was still fully loaded. He glanced then to the house. Cass Berryman and his friends were still inside. Joel grinned tightly. So far he and Amos had not been missed.

'All set,' the older man announced finally.

Joel turned immediately and, leading the sorrel, retraced his steps down the runway to the side door through which they had entered earlier. Halting, he made a careful check to be certain there was no one around, and then stepped into the open. The door was barely large enough to permit passage of the horses, but they managed, and shortly the two Kanes were mounted.

'Which way are we heading?' Amos asked.

'Need a good place to hide. It's too far to town. Got any ideas?'

The older man thought for a moment, nodded. 'That old trapper's shack, back up in the rimrocks. Nobody ever goes up there any more.'

'Just what we want,' Joel said. 'Let's go.'

V

An hour later they were high in the rock-studded country west of the valley. Joel had forgotten about the cabin until his father had brought it to mind, and, visualizing it and its location now, he was certain it would be an ideal place for Amos to hide until he could bring matters with Cass Berryman to a head. Just how he would manage to get the outlaws off the Circle K was still unclear in his mind. However, at the moment, his thoughts centered only on the will his father had made and its recovery. With it destroyed, he reasoned, the threat to Amos Kane's life would be removed – or at least diminished.

The next move would then be Berryman's, and ideally the outlaw and his crew would simply pull stakes and drift on to greener grazing, forgetting the Circle K. But

Joel had few illusions on that score. Cass Berryman had a good thing going for him on the Kane ranch, and he wouldn't toss it away without a bitter fight.

'Shack's on the other side of that shoulder,' Amos called.

Joel looked ahead. The narrow trail veered sharply to his left, cut its way through a narrow slash in a huge bulge of granite. If it came down to a war with the outlaws, here would be a good place to make a stand, he thought. A man with a rifle, well hidden in the rocks, could hold off a small army.

Rounding the corner, they broke into a small clearing covered with matted clumps of yellow mountain daisies. Set back on the far side, the stone and log cabin appeared half buried in the dark soil. Buckbrush, sage, scrub oak, and other shrubs crowded in from all points, giving the place a desolate, abandoned appearance.

Crossing over, they dismounted, and, while Amos went inside to have his look, Joel led the gray around to the rear and picketed him in the dense undergrowth where grass was plentiful. Returning, he found his father standing in the doorway.

'Nobody's been here for years.'

'Just the place we need,' Joel said, 'but don't take any chances. Stay inside and don't build a fire. Berryman will be hunting for us.'

'If I hear somebody coming, I'll take to the brush.'

'Do what you figure best. The main thing is not to be seen. Expect I'll be back about the middle of the afternoon.'

'Going to return to the ranch?'

Joel nodded. 'Aim to get that will. Any idea where Berryman keeps it?'

The older man clawed at his chin. 'Pretty sure he isn't carrying it on him. Most likely it's in that old desk of mine in the parlor. He took it over for his office. How're you going to get inside so's you can search with them there?'

'I figure they'll pull out and start looking for us as soon as they find we're gone. Shouldn't be anybody left but the cook, and

I can get by him.'

'Stoyers won't give you any trouble.'

'Maybe not, but I don't intend to give him the choice.' Joel turned to the sorrel, swung aboard. 'I'll bring back some grub and a couple of blankets.'

The older man's brows lifted. 'We going to stay here a spell?'

'Hard to say. Depends on Berryman. *Adiós.*'

'So long, Son,' Amos answered as Joel cut back to the trail. 'Take care.'

Joel halted, when he reached the foot of the rocky slope. It seemed unwise to move directly toward the ranch. Berryman could be aware of their escape by that hour and have men searching. He decided to keep well in the deep brush until he knew exactly how matters stood.

Accordingly, he swung right and began a circuitous approach. It was almost noon, and ordinarily the outlaws could be expected to be sitting down to their midday meal – but that wouldn't necessarily hold true, if someone had opened the storeroom door. If that had occurred, the hunt would already be under way.

Evidently it was. Kane realized it a short time later when he halted on a hill south of the buildings and looked into the yard. The horses were gone. Considering the hour, they should still be there unless...

'There he is!'

The voice came suddenly from the trees to his left. Instantly a pistol cracked, and Joel heard the clip of leaves as a bullet sped through the foliage beyond him. He threw a glance to the side as he spurred around. The shot had come from Bill Taney. A short distance behind the husky outlaw, Berryman, and Dobe Rivera were wheeling their horses about in response to Bill's shout. He saw nothing of the fourth outlaw, Clete Jordan.

He wasted no time locating the man. He'd be somewhere nearby, little doubt of that. Heading the sorrel into the dense brush, he sent him plunging forward, away from the trail that led toward the cabin where Amos hid. More gunshots crackled through the hot stillness, but he didn't hear the snap of bullets, so he guessed the outlaws were shooting blindly.

Abruptly he broke out of the thick undergrowth into a long, twisting wash. He would be an open target there and immediately veered the sorrel to the right, topped out the rim of the slash, and raced on, driving hard for a grove of trees a hundred yards distant. It was going to be close. Reaching down, he pulled the rifle from its boot. Clamping the stock of the weapon under his arm, he levered a shell into the chamber and looked back. Taney and the missing Jordan were just appearing above the edge of the wash. Taking quick aim, he pressed off a shot.

Sand spurted a few paces in front of the men, and both swerved hastily. Joel grinned, levered another cartridge into the rifle. He'd spoiled their opportunity.

He heard Cass Berryman's voice just as he entered the grove, glanced back. All four outlaws were streaming across the flat.

Berryman was waving his arms, shouting for them to split up, box him in. Kane snapped another bullet into the general direction of the oncoming men, saw the *vaquero* jerk to the right as the slug droned by him. They hadn't figured on his having a weapon, and this fact was laying a caution upon them.

He lost sight of them a moment later, when the trees closed in behind him, and immediately began to slow the sorrel's rush while he tried to figure his best move. He'd led them away from the trail into the rimrocks, and he felt now that Amos would be in no danger. To keep going straight on, to the opposite side of the ranch, seemed the logical course.

Spurring the sorrel again, he drove on, winding in and out of the pines, hoping the outlaws had not lost sight of him entirely. Reaching the upper end of the grove, he slowed and looked back. Almost immediately a gunshot flatted across the hush, and again he heard the sharp clipping of a bullet tearing through the brush. He had cut it a little too thin.

He felt his nerves tighten as he sent the sorrel hurrying on. Half turning in the saddle, he fired another shot at the blurred shapes coming through the shadows. A flurry of pistol shots was his answer, but only one bullet sounded near.

Suddenly he was again in the open, racing across a narrow, almost level field. On the far side was another stand of pines that ran all the way to the cliffs on one side, to the valley on the other. He would never have a better chance to shake the outlaws.

Leaning forward on the straining red, he deliberately veered toward the lower end of the trees, as if heading downslope into the valley. A fresh burst of shots broke out at that moment, but he paid no heed. They had seen him and that was what he wanted.

He gained the trees, continued on down-grade until he was well within the grove and entirely hidden. He swerved sharply then, altering his course completely, and began to double back toward the cliffs. He followed that procedure for a short distance, allowing the heaving sorrel to move at a fast walk, finally cutting back at right angles through the grove until he reached its fringe.

Dismounting, he worked his way through the brush until he could see the open field. Far below, the outlaws were just entering the trees. They had angled across the flat, hoping to cut down his lead by taking a more direct line. When they didn't find him, they would assume him to still be ahead, trying to reach the valley. Kane heaved a sigh. Each step was taking them farther from the ranch. He could now return and carry out his search for Amos Kane's will without fear of interruption.

VI

He rode into the ranch from the east side and hid the sorrel in a strip of tamarisk Amos had planted years ago for a windbreak. No sounds were coming from the house, and Joel wondered briefly if Stoyers, the cook, had gone – perhaps to town for supplies. If so, he would be in luck, but he had his doubts about it.

Working his way to the corner of the house, where he had a grand view of the yard and the barn standing at its far end, he halted. There was no sign of the hostlers either, and that didn't seem normal. He didn't believe he had struck either man hard enough to cause serious injury, and both should be about. Could they be inside the main house?

It was a possibility, and a risk he'd have to accept. He couldn't afford to delay a search of the house for long. Eventually Cass Berryman and his men would return. Dropping back, Joel made his way along the east wall of the house to one of the bedrooms. The window was open, but a square of wire had been tacked on the outer frame to ward off insects. He spent another ten minutes quietly prying out the tacks and removing the screen. That finally done, he listened to be certain he had aroused no one. Finally satisfied his efforts had gone unnoticed, he hoisted himself through the opening and into the room.

Again he paused to listen. The place was in dead silence, and the conviction grew within him that Ben Stoyers was absent. Crossing to a door that led into a hallway, he entered and followed the corridor to where it opened into the parlor. Amos had said the will would most likely be found in the old rolltop desk now used by Berryman. He spotted it, standing against the back wall and, moving to it, immediately began a search of its drawers and hinged compartments.

The distant pound of a hammer brought him up short. He stepped back to the hallway and listened, while he tried to locate the sound. Coming from the barn, he decided, likely one of the hostlers. There was no threat there as long as the man continued his labors.

Returning to the desk, he resumed his inspection, carefully checking every paper, even going through the pages of several account books in hopes Berryman had secreted the will in that manner. He found nothing other than an indication of the outlaw's business ability – and that he was salting money away in the Cedar River bank.

At a loss as to where to look next, Joel returned to the hall. The bedroom – the one used by Cass Berryman. He crossed to the nearest, began to go through the dresser drawers, the clothing hanging in the closet – nothing.

Unsure as to which were Berryman's quarters, he followed a similar procedure in the adjoining room. There he found his pistol, taken from him earlier by Clete Jordan, but no more than that. Holstering his weapon, he stood in the center of the dimly lit room to think. He had searched all the logical places and turned up nothing. He began to wonder if it wasn't likely Cass Berryman carried the paper on his person. It didn't seem possible, yet – Kane shook his head. The will was hidden somewhere in the house – it had to be. Wheeling, he went back to the first bedroom, since the clothing there appeared to be that of the red-haired outlaw leader. He'd have to move fast, however. Time was running out, and his luck wouldn't hold indefinitely.

Again he ransacked the drawers, examined each item of clothing, even to checking the insides of three pairs of boots he discovered on a shelf. To no avail. He turned to the bed, pulled it apart, paying particular attention to the mattress. Again a blank. From there he went to the carpet tacked to the floor and felt along its edge for a bulge while he listened for the crackle of paper. That, too, proved fruitless, and he next removed the framed pictures hanging on the wall and checked them carefully. When this also failed to turn up the missing paper, he abandoned the bedroom and went once more to the parlor.

He hadn't given the furniture a going over, he realized, and at once began a thorough investigation of the chair bottoms, the springs in the dust-covered couch, the underside of the heavy lion-footed table. A braided rug was spread on the floor, and, heaving the furniture to one side, he kicked it into a heap. There was nothing hidden beneath it, either.

He paused and studied the desk, wishing now he had asked his father about secret drawers or compartments in the massive old piece. Most desks like this contained some, he knew, each elaborately concealed in an unlikely spot. With that in mind he began to go over the desk, removing drawers, checking for false bottoms, thrusting his hand deeply into vacated slots for a second container. Eventually he found it – a smaller drawer that fell into place when the front member was entirely removed. It was filled with folded papers and a few gold coins. Hurriedly he dumped it all on the desk and then, one by one, began to unfold and read the yellowing sheets. Deeds, bills of sale, letters – but no will.

Disappointed, he returned the papers and money to their container, reset it, and continued the search. There could be a second secret compartment, but he knew it was a slim possibility. He didn't like the thought of admitting it, but the fact that the will was not in the house was becoming clearly evident. Either Cass Berryman was carrying it or – Joel Kane's thoughts came to a full stop. A faint, scraping sound had registered on his consciousness. He felt a slight prickling along his spine. He'd pushed his luck too far. Arms hanging at his sides, he slowly turned to face the doorway.

Ben Stoyers, a shotgun cocked and ready in his hands, stared at him. Stoyers said: 'What the hell do you think you're doing?'

The old man's eyes were deep-set, hard. He took a short step into the room, glanced about at the disorder and confusion. Joel moved slightly. Stoyers was instantly alert.

'Get your hands up ... away from that pistol!' he barked, waggling the shotgun threateningly.

Kane raised his arms slowly. 'I'm Joel ... Amos's son.'

'I know that. What's it got to do with your being here, tearing the place to pieces?'

'You're Pa's friend ... been with him a long

time, he said.'

Ben Stoyers only watched in his sharp, bird-like way.

'I'm trying to help him.'

'Against Berryman?'

Joel nodded. 'You know the deal and what they're trying to do to him. I'm going to stop it.'

The old cook was silent for a time. Then: 'Where's he now?'

'Hid out where they can't find him. Soon as I get what I want, I'm moving in on Berryman and his bunch and driving them off the place.'

Stoyers grunted. 'Bit yourself off a big chaw.'

'I'll get help, if I have to.'

'From who? The old man hasn't got any friends.'

'I'm doing it, not him,' Joel replied, vaguely angered. He stirred impatiently. Time was slipping by and with it his margin of safety – Berryman and the others would be returning.

Stoyers jerked his head at the room in general. 'You looking for something?'

'That will Pa's signed, giving everything to Cass Berryman when he's dead.'

'It's not here. He keeps it safe in the bank,' Stoyers broke in, and then bit off his words as if he had spoken more than he intended.

'The bank,' Kane murmured. He hadn't given that possibility any thought, but it stood to reason. Berryman had gone to great lengths in every other way to make things appear legal and above board.

'Amos change his mind?'

The question was clearly unnecessary, but Joel said: 'He has. Way it stands now Berryman's in a hurry to see him dead so's he can take over. Once I get that will back and destroy it, he won't have a reason.'

'Won't make any difference to Cass. He's got the place, and he'll hang onto it. Your pa's signing that paper just made it easy for him ... kept it all legal-like.'

'He can *try* hanging onto it,' Joel corrected quietly. 'And he'll be doing it without any real claim.' He studied the old man for a moment, then said: 'Where do you stand, Ben?'

'What's that mean?'

'Pa said he figured you for a friend, only you were stringing along with Berryman and his bunch because you didn't have much choice.'

'About the size of it,' the cook said with a shrug. 'Man looks out for himself. Reckon I was working for Amos a long time before Cass and his boys came along.'

'That means you're still siding him?'

Stoyers lowered the shotgun. 'Reckon it does.'

Joel Kane sighed and lowered his arms. Undoubtedly the outlaws were close by at that moment, but he could leave now. He knew where to find what he sought.

'You want to help?' he asked, stepping to the doorway where he could better listen for approaching horses.

'Sure.'

'Better understand what it'll mean. Like

you said, Berryman won't give up easy. Going to be some people hurt before it's over with.'

'I'm old enough to know that. What do you want me to do?'

'Best you get out of here. Berryman learns you've thrown in with Pa and me, your life won't be worth much.'

'Where'll I go?'

'To where Pa's hid out. Take along some grub and a couple of blankets ... and that scatter-gun. How about the two men in the barn?'

'Berryman brought them here.'

'Leaves them out. Can you get away without them knowing about it?'

Stoyers bobbed his head. 'Expect I can manage. Where's Amos at?'

'Old trapper's cabin ... south end of the rimrocks. Take the trail below...'

'I know where it is. I've done some hunting up there, off and on. Where'll you be?'

'Paying the bank a call. Once I get my hands on that will, we'll give Berryman a chance to pull out. If he doesn't, we'll drive him off.'

'Take more'n you and Amos ... and me.'

'Could be.'

'You thinking about bringing in the law?'

'If I have to.'

Stoyers shook his head. 'That's not such a smart idea. Way things have been run around here, I doubt if Amos'll want the law poking into how he gets his beef and what he does with it.'

'That's Berryman's doings, not Pa's.'

'Proving it won't be easy. Amos's name is on the bills of sale.'

Joel swore softly. Berryman was a careful man, too. He had taken pains to cover all possible problems. It would be hard to convince people Amos did not participate in the rustling that went on – more difficult yet to make them believe he was powerless to stop it. Loner that he was, he was certain to be misjudged. But all that'd come later; there were immediate things now to be handled.

Kane moved into the hallway. 'Got to get

out of here before Berryman and the others show up. Best you do the same,' he said, walking hurriedly toward the bedroom where he had entered.

Stoyers trailed him down the hall. 'Where'll we meet you?'

'Stay at the cabin. I'll come there as soon as I've finished my business with the bank.'

The cook nodded.

Joel thrust a leg through the window, then hesitated. 'Be careful leaving here. Don't let anybody follow you.'

Stoyers grinned. 'Don't go worrying about me,' he said.

VII

Very little of Cedar River was familiar to Joel Kane. He had been in the town only a few times, and during his early childhood at that. As he turned into the single main street, he glanced about curiously: several saloons, a café or two, barber, harness and gun store, and all the other shops and offices found in similar settlements scattered across the West. *They all look alike,* he thought, singling out the bank and angling toward the hitch rack fronting it.

Halting, he dismounted and wrapped the sorrel's reins around the crossbar and then swung his eyes back over the way he had come. Across the dusty, rutted strip and down a few doors the town's marshal had moved out onto the walk and was regarding him with quiet interest. Joel returned the lawman's gaze, nodded slightly, turned, and entered the bank.

Except for an elderly man wearing steel-rimmed spectacles and a green eye shade in the teller's cage and a well-dressed individual seated at a desk, the place was deserted. It would be Henry Testman at the desk, Joel guessed, and made his way to that point.

The banker, sallow-faced and clad in a soft gray suit, glanced up as Kane halted in front of the desk. 'Something I can do for you?'

Joel said: 'You Henry Testman?'

The man nodded cautiously.

Kane offered his hand. 'I'm Joel Kane ... Amos's son. Been away for a spell.'

Testman frowned, shook hands limply. 'Son?' he repeated, and then added: 'Yes, I remember now. How long ago was it?'

'Ten years, more or less.'

Testman motioned at a chair. Kane drew it up next to the desk and sat down. The banker cocked his head to one side. 'What brought you back?'

There was something about the banker's attitude that rubbed Joel wrong. He would have to overlook it, he realized. He couldn't afford to antagonize Testman. He shrugged. 'Man comes home ... eventually.'

Testman said: 'Yes, I suppose so. What can I do for you?'

Bankers, he'd learned, liked the indirect approach. 'Looking for information mostly ... sort of getting acquainted again,' he said. 'Pa and I were talking this morning. Said he'd made out a will.'

Henry Testman nodded.

'I'd like to have a look at it.'

The banker settled back, bridged his fingers, and frowned. 'Why?'

'Pa's getting old. Not too sure what he put in it.'

'He signed it.'

'I know that, but like I said he's getting pretty old and doesn't think too good.' Joel paused. He was treading on thin ice. The banker could get angry, flatly refuse his request, but he had to risk it. 'There some reason why you don't want me to see it?' he demanded suspiciously.

Testman leaned forward quickly and shook his head. 'Of course not, only ... well, it's not customary. A will is a private paper.'

'He's my pa,' Joel said. 'He sent me. If you don't believe that, saddle up, and we'll ride out and ask him.'

'No need,' the banker said wearily. Reaching out, he pulled open a drawer, removed a leather folder, and began to sort through a thick sheaf of papers. Selecting one, he handed it to Kane. 'Afraid you're going to be disappointed,' he said. 'Won't find your name in there.'

'That's what Pa told me,' Joel replied, and unfolded the sheet.

It was as Amos had said: everything had been signed over to Cass Berryman. Kane studied the document briefly, then refolded it, and thrust it into his shirt pocket.

'Better take this along. Pa's aiming to make some changes.'

Henry Testman came forward angrily. 'You can't do that!'

'Why can't I? Belongs to my pa. He wants it.'

'But he didn't leave it with me. It's somebody else's property!'

'Cass Berryman's?'

'Matter of fact, yes. He entrusted it to me ... to the bank ... for safekeeping. I can't turn it over to you unless he says so.'

'Not his property,' Kane said evenly.

'It is!' Testman snapped. 'If you walk out

of here with it, it will be robbery ... the same thing as a bank hold-up.'

The banker's voice had lifted sharply. The teller moved out from behind his screened cubicle and glanced toward the door. Joel drew his pistol and rose to his feet.

'Forget it,' he warned the clerk, then brought his attention back to Testman. 'No reason to get riled up about this. Man has a right to change his own will. If you're worried about Berryman, make out some sort of receipt, and I'll sign it.'

'I don't want a receipt... I want that document back!'

'We'll leave it up to Pa. If he wants you to have it, I'll bring it back ... after he's through making his changes.'

'No!'

Joel looked keenly at the banker. 'Maybe you don't want him changing it. Maybe you want it left just like it is. You got a deal going with Cass Berryman?'

Testman's face darkened. 'That's neither here nor there. You've got no right to take that paper.'

'Got every right,' Joel drawled. 'And if you're smart, you'll just sit tight and forget it.'

'Trouble here, Henry?'

Joel whirled at the question. The town's lawman was standing inside the doorway. A tall, lean man with iron-gray hair, he had entered so quietly Kane had heard nothing.

The lawman saw the pistol in Joel's hand. His jaw settled into a firm line and his eyes narrowed. 'This is a hold-up?' he asked coolly.

Kane shook his head. 'Just picking up a paper for my pa, Marshal.'

'Why the gun?'

'It's a hold-up, Tom.' Testman broke in before Joel could answer. 'Says he's Amos Kane's boy. Maybe he is, maybe he's not. Forced me to hand over the old man's will.'

'Forced?'

Testman, on his feet, pointed to the weapon in Joel's hand. 'Why do you think he's holding that?'

The marshal placed his flat gaze on Kane.

'Can't see as it matters what you're after. Using a gun to get it makes it a hold-up. Now, put that weapon away and give Testman back that paper.'

'It's important that I don't,' Joel said. 'You want to hear my side of it?' He had considered laying the whole story of Berryman's duplicity before the law and asking for help, if it became necessary. This could be the opportune moment.

'Not interested,' the marshal said. 'Only thing I want is to see you put that iron in its holster, and fork over that paper.'

'Then what?'

'Then we're taking a walk over to my jail. I'm putting you under arrest, while I get to the bottom of this.'

'Arrest! On what charge?'

'You've heard it ... hold-up.'

Impatience ripped through Kane. 'Not a hold-up, Marshal, and you know it. If you want to do something, get on your horse and go back to the Circle K with me. That's where some law's needed.'

'What's wrong out there?'

'He's all heated up because his pa's leaving the ranch to Cass Berryman,' Testman offered. 'He ran off ten years ago ... left the old man flat. Berryman stepped in and has been looking after things all this time. Now he's come back, wanting his share.'

The lawman nodded thoughtfully. 'That the way of it? You pull out like Henry says and just now come back?'

'He's right...'

'That will leave everything to Berryman?'

'It does, but that's not the reason I'm here. Pa sent for me. He's in trouble.'

'Why would Amos Kane send for him?' Testman persisted. 'He disowned him after he left. Be the last man he'd go to for help ... if he *was* in trouble, seems to me he'd go to you.'

'Makes sense,' the lawman agreed.

'How do you know?' Joel demanded. 'You ever drop by the Circle K, see how things were going?'

'Well, can't say as I have. Just never had no

reason to, and your pa ... he ain't the friend-
liest man I ever met.'

'Then you don't know...?'

'I know just one thing, Kane,' the lawman
said, his voice going brittle, 'you'd better do
like I tell you, or you're in real trouble,
because I'm not letting you walk out of here.'

'I'm walking out, all right,' Joel said,
abruptly out of patience. He brought up his
pistol, leveled it at the old lawman. 'Get over
here with Testman. You, too,' he added,
motioning to the teller.

The two men moved slowly up beside the
banker's desk. Beyond them the door to a
closet stood partly open.

'In there,' Kane said crisply.

Testman and the clerk began to back slowly
toward the small room; the lawman did not
stir. Temper finally got the best of Kane. He
stepped in close, lifted the older man's pistol
from its holster, flung it into a corner.

'Move ... damn you!' he snarled. 'I don't
want trouble with you!'

The lawman stared at Joel for several

moments and then began to retreat with the others. 'You've already got trouble, mister,' he said. 'Plenty.'

There was no key for the closet door. Kane dragged up a chair, wedged it under the knob, blocking it securely. Turning then, he left the bank and mounted the sorrel. Swinging off into the street, he shook his head. *Now I've got the law and the outlaws both gunning for my hide,* he thought.

VIII

The sun was well on its westward swing, when Joel Kane reached the trail leading to the rimrocks. He was feeling much better. The will was in his possession, thus removing the immediate threat to Amos Kane's life, and now it would be only a matter of time until Berryman and his outlaw following could be driven from the Circle K. He regretted the measures he had been compelled to take where the marshal of Cedar River was concerned. He had never been at odds with the law, and he didn't like the idea – but he had been given no choice. Henry Testman had made an issue of surrendering the will, either because of some arrangement he had with Cass Berryman, or possibly due to a sense of loyalty to what he considered his duty as a banker. Joel was uncertain which. Regardless, when it was all cleared up, he'd go to the old lawman and explain why he had been forced to act as he did. With his father's backing and a presentation of the facts concerning Berryman, he should be able to make the marshal understand.

The sorrel, tired from the long day, picked his way slowly up the rock-studded path. Joel did not push him. It would be too late, when he reached the cabin, to do anything but rest anyway, and there was no point in punishing the big red. He touched his pocket, reassuring himself that the will was there. He'd let Amos tear it up, burn it. It would give Amos pleasure and perhaps act as a sort of stimulant for the job that lay ahead. Joel still had no definite plan of action in mind. He guessed it would be a good idea to talk things over with Amos and Ben Stoyers, get their ideas, and then start things rolling in the morning. He hoped the old cook had remembered to bring along some grub. He hadn't eaten since morning and was feeling the need for food.

At the first granite ledge the sorrel halted, unsure of the rain-washed surface. Joel swung down, intending to lead the red across its narrow width. At that moment he heard a faint halloo coming from below, and halted. Frowning, he moved to the edge of the ledge and studied the rolling, brushy contours of the distant valley.

Motion to the south caught his eyes – several slow-moving dots winding in and out of the gray-green undergrowth. Berryman and his men, he decided, continuing the search. More dots appeared, working now toward a central point. Methodically he counted them. Ten riders in all.

A hard grin pulled at his lips. These men weren't outlaws; this was a posse from Cedar River. The marshal had lost no time organizing a pursuit. It looked as if the old lawman was following no specific trail, however, but was hunting blind – he was now swinging his men north, away from the rimrock country.

He had nothing to fear, Joel concluded. The posse would search until darkness fell and then give it up. They might possibly return at daylight, depending on how great the injury to the marshal's pride had been and how strong were his powers of persuasion. Thinking about it, Kane hoped they would come again; perhaps he could devise a plan whereby he would lead Berryman and his followers into the hands of the posse. Amos could then lay the facts before the marshal and press whatever charges he desired.

Charges? Joel considered that thought. *What charges?* That Berryman had been unnecessarily hard on him? That he planned to murder him in order to take over the Circle

K? They would be difficult to prove, and any verification from Joel would be discounted, just as it had been in the bank – the son, returning home and resenting the fact that an outsider was to inherit his father's property. He would have to handle Berryman himself, Joel realized. It would be best to keep the law out of it, at least until he'd made the first move and had the outlaws on the defensive.

The posse had all but disappeared, cutting to the east now. The ranch lay in that direction and, twenty miles beyond it, the town itself. Chances were better than good that the lawman and his men would encounter Berryman somewhere along the way. He wondered what the outlaw would tell the marshal when he learned they both sought the same fugitive. It would be a good story; Berryman was a smooth one to deal with.

Tugging at the leathers, he led the sorrel on across the ledge, remounted, and continued up the steep trail. A short time later he broke out onto another bench and saw the shoulder of rock beyond which the cabin stood. *Almost there,* he thought with relief. In a few more minutes he'd be out of the saddle and easing his tired muscles while he satisfied the hunger now gnawing at him. He hoped Ben Stoyers had coffee ready.

Amos and the old cook had heeded his warning. The shack appeared as deserted as ever. Joel rode in slowly, anxious to arrive, yet restrained as always by an inner instinct that, throughout his life, had unremittingly refused to accept any situation at face value. As he had done many times in the past, he tried to brush aside the caution, telling himself that the evident absence of life, the lack of greeting, was to be expected, that it was something of his own doing, since he had told both men to remain hidden, taking no chances. But the uneasiness persisted. He reached the edge of the clearing, the sorrel moving in slow, weary steps, and halted, eyes on the closed door. He sat for a moment, studying the weather-beaten panel, and then, ignoring his misgivings, he swung down. Ground reining the sorrel, he hitched at his gun belt and started for the door.

'Joel, trap!'

The muffled warning brought him up short. He heard something fall inside the cabin and clawed for his pistol just as another sound came from his left. He spun fast to see Bill Taney and the *vaquero* break suddenly from a screen of brush.

Kane lunged to one side as Taney fired. The bullet thudded into the front of the cabin, sending up a puff of dust. Joel, snapping a quick reply at the outlaw, whirled again. Directly ahead was Berryman and not far from him, Clete Jordan. They were trying to box him in, push him back against the shack.

Escape on the sorrel was out of the question. He leaped aside and ducked behind a clump of sage, going full length and rolling fast until he was in the deep shadow of a scrub cedar.

'Get him ... god-damn it!' Berryman yelled. 'He's in that brush!'

Guns crackled, drowning the outlaw's strident command. Bullets smashed into the sage, churning the feathery leaves. Crawling, Joel gained the shelter of a rocky ledge, drew himself to a crouch. He couldn't see the outlaws, but guessed they were closing in on the clump of sage, expecting him to be there.

He darted off, running low and quiet, circling in behind the cabin. There was no way he could return to the sorrel, but Amos's horse was picketed in the undergrowth back of the shack. If he could reach – he caught sight of the gray. The horse was thirty feet away, head lifted, ears pricked forward as he looked curiously at Kane's crouched shape. Keeping low, Joel hurried on.

'He ain't here!'

Bill Taney's voice was shot with surprise. There was a muffled curse and then Berryman's impatient shout: 'Got to be there! I saw him jump in behind that bush ... and with all that shooting! Look again!'

'Must've missed him. He sure ain't here!'

'Doubt that.' Cass Berryman's tone was less insistent. 'Bound to have winged him, so keep hunting. He can't have gone far.'

Joel reached the gray, jerked the reins loose. He started to swing onto the saddle, but thought better of it. Mounted, he would be above the brush and easily seen.

Leading the horse, he dropped back another ten yards and then, believing himself well screened, stepped into the saddle. Instantly a gunshot blasted through the quiet, and he felt the shock of a bullet searing across his shoulders.

'Over here! Over here!' Clete Jordan's voice shouted.

Throwing himself forward in the saddle, Joel dug spurs into the gray's flanks and pointed him for the higher ledges of the rimrocks. The gray began to labor on the rough upgrade almost at once. Kane swore in frustration; the horse had no bottom – he'd go down in another hundred yards at that pace. He swore again, wishing he had the sorrel; tired as he was, the big red at his worst was twice as good as the gray.

He looked back. Berryman and the others were somewhere below. They couldn't be far, but the rocky outcroppings and dense under-growth hid them from view. He could hear them shouting, and now and then came the rattle of displaced gravel and the dry slap of brush.

The trail veered to the right, breaking its steep ascent, and leveled off on a sparsely grassed shelf. Immediately the gray caught his wind, picked up speed, and for a brief time gained rapidly on the pursuing outlaws. And then again the path turned upward, now following a narrow gash in the granite face of the mountain. Joel began to feel the sting of the wound across his shoulders. With one hand he reached around to explore it gingerly. The skin was barely broken, al-though there was considerable blood. Jor-dan's bullet had just skimmed his body, slic-ing a shallow furrow in its flight. If the slug had been a half inch lower, he'd be back at the cabin helpless, possibly dead.

Near the top of the crevice the gray stumbled, churned his hoofs to regain balance, and sent a quantity of loose rock cascading onto the ledge below. Yells went up, and a solitary shot echoed through the gathering darkness. Kane heard no thud of a bullet and guessed that whoever'd fired had simply aimed in the general direction of the racket. He stared ahead. The gray was beginning to wilt and would need rest at once. Kane could see no break in the trail. It continued to climb seemingly straight up as it pointed for the upper crests and ridges.

Berryman and his men were still hidden from view, and the sounds of their coming seemed more distant. He'd almost lost them at the gash when he turned off, he realized, and they'd lost time doubling back. If the gray hadn't stumbled and set off a disturbance, he might have gotten into the clear. But that didn't help now. The gray had to be given a few minutes' rest – and, besides, he must somehow get back to the cabin. Amos and Ben Stoyers were probably prisoners, likely hurt. Something had happened inside the shack when Amos had yelled his warning. If Joel could turn off the trail, hide and allow the outlaws to bypass him, he could cut back down the mountain. Under cover of darkness it wouldn't be too difficult. Anxiously, he again peered ahead. The trail ran on, hemmed in on both sides by sheer rock.

He wondered how Berryman had found Amos. The last he'd seen of the outlaws they were far off in another direction. It had been by sheer accident, he supposed – or possibly Berryman had known of the cabin and had led his men there on an outside chance he'd find the Kanes. If so, the hunch had certainly paid off for him.

A darker area loomed up to his left. Hope rose within him, and he strained his eyes to determine the nature of the break in the otherwise solid wall of rock. A narrow cañon, filled with thick-growing piñon trees which apparently extended the complete depth of the slash. The trees were not large but were so crowded they formed an almost impenetrable screen.

Using spurs, he goaded the winded gray to a faster pace. No turnoff was apparent, and, if he could make the swing without being seen by the outlaws, they would simply assume that he had continued on toward the summit. Reaching the draw, he cut the gray around and broke into the first of the piñons. Brush crowded the ground beneath the trees, and for the first dozen strides the horse had little easier going than on the steep trail, but shortly the clumps of scrub oak and sage thinned out and progress became much simpler.

He rode the gray well back into the pocket of the cañon and halted. Staying in the saddle, he turned to watch. The piñons were like a solid green wall, shutting off all except what was immediately before him. Dissatisfied, he slipped from the saddle, anchored the gray, and made his way forward until he could look upon the trail.

The outlaws were only minutes behind him. He heard first the sharp click of a metal shoe against stone and then the dry squeak of leather. Kane tried to locate them in the darkness, but the moon was not yet strong, and the men were evidently beyond the mouth of the cañon.

Cass Berryman's voice broke the hush. 'Ought to be pulling up on him. That gray's wind-broken. Hasn't got it in him to do much hard climbing.'

'That why we aren't hearing him?' Taney asked. 'Reckon he could've turned off, given us the slip?'

'Turned off where?' Berryman's voice was ragged, impatient.

One of the others said something in a low voice – the *vaquero*, Joel thought – but he couldn't make out the words. That left Jordan to account for. The sound of their passage was clear now, and a moment later he saw the upper portion of their bodies silhouetted against the faint, rising glow. Three riders only. Where was Clete Jordan?

'Be a damn' good place for him to be hiding,' Bill Taney said, pulling to a stop abreast the cañon. 'Hard to find anything in there.'

The others halted.

Berryman said: 'It's worth a look.' Then:

'Where the hell's Clete?'

'He tried a swing to the west ... figured Kane could've dodged that way.'

'Ought to be showing up. Nothing but cliffs through there. Man can't get to the top unless he sticks to the trail.'

'He knows that. He'll be catching up. Want me to take a sashay through the trees while we're waiting?'

Joel threw a hasty glance around. Taney was certain to spot the gray. He'd best move farther back into the grove, try to find taller growth. He turned, felt his foot strike against a stone. A thought passed through his mind, and, leaning over, he picked up the rock. It might work. Moving forward to where he had room, he threw the stone uptrail as hard as he could. It fell with a hollow thud, creating a small gravel slide.

Berryman swore. 'He's not in there. Still ahead of us.'

'Not far either,' Bill Taney replied. 'We go on or wait for Clete?'

'Keep going. Sounded like we're pretty

close. Jordan'll find us.'

Immediately Joel heard the sound of their horses as they resumed the trail. He grinned into the pale night. The outlaws had fallen for a trick as old as Indian fighting itself. He'd give them a couple of minutes and head back for the cabin. Jordan? He'd have to go carefully. The thin-faced gunman was below him somewhere, probably on the trail now. While Joel didn't remember much about the mountain, he knew Berryman had been correct in saying it was impossible to reach the summit except by the path. Sheer rock walls blocked every other access. Jordan would have been forced to cut down off the slope, get on the trail.

Kane returned to the gray and mounted. He sat out a long five minutes, wishing Jordan would appear and ride on by. It would make matters much simpler. He gave it another three minutes and concluded he could delay no longer. He'd need plenty of time, once he reached the cabin, to get Amos and Ben Stoyers out of the shack and onto horses – and well down the trail. And if either of the men was injured...

He touched the gray lightly and started down the cañon. It would be smart to stay off the path as much as possible, do his traveling on the shoulder, even if it was slower. In that way he stood a chance of seeing the outlaw before being seen.

A sound to his right brought Kane to a sudden halt. He pivoted and saw Clete Jordan. The outlaw's features registered surprise, and Joel realized the man was as startled as he.

Jordan reacted instantly. His hand swept down for the pistol on his hip. Kane was equally fast, but, wanting no gunshot echoing across the mountain to summon Berryman and the others, launched himself from the saddle. He hit the outlaw with solid force and threw his arms around Jordan's body. Together they went to the ground, thrashing wildly. Joel, on top, fought to keep his grip around Jordan, knowing he must prevent the man from drawing his weapon. But Clete was no newcomer to the rough-and-tumble way of combat. He began to twist, to use his legs, his head. Kane felt his grasp slipping.

Gasping for breath, Joel managed to get his knees under him. He drew himself up slightly and lifted Jordan. Gathering strength, he lunged forward, smashing Jordan to the ground beneath him. Jordan's wind exploded in a gusty blast, and for a brief instant his efforts suspended. Joel instantly released his grip and drove a balled fist into the outlaw's jaw. Clete groaned, struggled to pull away. Merciless, Kane hammered at his head, his neck and face. Jordan managed to get to his hands and knees. Joel drew himself upright and, standing over the outlaw, drove him flat with a down-sledging blow. Jordan went limp.

Breathing hard, Kane stared at the unconscious man for several moments and then, turning, staggered to where the gray waited. Pulling himself into the saddle, he headed downgrade for the cabin.

IX

Joel swept into the flat at a gallop. Time was too short to worry about noise. He doubted if Cass Berryman and the two men with him, far up on the side of the mountain, could hear the gray anyway. As for Clete Jordan, it didn't matter.

The cabin stood silently in the now bright moonlight, and Joel felt his fears rise again. Amos could be dead. The outlaws could have injured him fatally and thus completed the job they had planned for Mud Lake. Anxious, he swerved the gray in beside the sorrel, leaped to the ground.

'Pa!' he shouted hoarsely, and rushed for the door.

He booted the panel open, then paused. A shaft of silver light reached into the small room and fell across the form of Amos Kane, crumpled in a back corner. A rag was across the lower half of his face, and his hands were bound behind him. Blood crusted his forehead in a ragged streak, but his eyes were open and greeted Joel with a bright feverishness.

'Pa,' Joel said again, relief flowing through him. Recalling the situation, he added hurriedly: 'We've got to get out of here quick.'

He stepped into the cabin – and felt the hard, round muzzle of a rifle jab into his back. Caught off guard, Joel froze while his mind raced to find an understanding.

'Step right in, Mister Kane. Make yourself to home.'

Ben Stoyers.

Joel, arms raised, wheeled slowly. He had the answer now as to how Berryman had found Amos. Stoyers was a double-crosser: he'd been one of the outlaw's crowd all along.

'You sneaking bastard!' Joel snarled. 'This is the way you pay back a man who's been your friend, given you a job...'

'Friend?' Stoyers echoed scornfully. 'He

ain't my friend! He's nobody's friend!'

'Fed you, furnished you with a place to stay, and paid you good money for what you did.'

'If he'd paid me a thousand dollars a day, it wouldn't have been enough! Working for him's like being a slave.'

'You could have quit ... walked off.'

The old cook swallowed hard, but he did not look away. 'Maybe, only I...'

'Only you knew you wouldn't get another job as good as the one you had. Nobody'd hire you.'

'Nothing good about it,' Stoyers muttered. 'Up, working daylight till dark. Taking his cussedness, letting him wipe his boots on me ... but I knew my day was coming.'

'And to get it you sold him out to Berryman. When did you decide to do that, Ben? When you saw me at the house?'

Stoyers laughed. 'A long time before that, mister. Made my mind up with Cass a couple of years ago. How do you figure he was able to keep tabs on old Amos so good?

Was me, watching close, letting Cass know what was going on all the time.'

Amos Kane stirred weakly, moaned.

Joel glanced at him, then back to the cook. 'Take that gag off him. No need for it now.'

Ben Stoyers wagged his head. 'Nope, just leave him be. I'm kind of enjoying myself, watching him squirm around.'

'He's hurt. At least, let me look at his wound.'

'Doesn't amount to anything. Just a little rap on the head. Cass and the boys'll be coming along in a minute anyway.'

That same thought had entered Joel's mind. He studied Stoyers quietly, calculating his chances of overcoming the man. If anything was to be done, it would have to be done quickly.

Stoyers, little more than an arm's length away, returned his stare with a crooked grin. He shifted his rifle. 'Thinking about jumping me ... that it?'

Kane shrugged. 'Be a fool to try ... with you standing there pointing that gun at me.'

'For a fact. I'd blow a hole in your guts big enough to walk through.'

Amos groaned again. Joel, sweat beading his brow, swore harshly. 'You've to let me take that gag off. He's having trouble breathing.'

Stoyers glanced at the elder Kane uncertainly.

'No risk for you as long as you're holding that rifle,' Joel pressed.

Abruptly the cook nodded. 'All right ... but first you turn yourself around. And keep your hands high.'

Joel wheeled slowly. He heard a slight sound as Stoyers stepped forward, then felt a lessening of weight on his hip as his pistol was removed from its holster.

'Go ahead,' the older man said then. 'But you move slow and easy. I'm a mite nervous.'

Kane crossed to his father's side and hurriedly pulled the gag loose. Amos stared up at him through dazed eyes.

'Joel?'

'It's me all right, Pa. You're going to be fine now.'

'Was afraid they'd caught you, too.'

Ben Stoyers cackled. 'They have, old man. We've got you both.'

Amos frowned. 'Who's that?' he asked, trying to focus his gaze.

'Stoyers,' Joel answered. In the pale glow of the moonlight that sifted into the cabin, Amos appeared very old – and very tired. The blow on his head had weakened him and left him slightly addled.

'Ben?' he said as if finding it hard to believe.

'He's sided with Berryman, Pa. He's no friend.'

Amos stirred wearily. 'Never figured Ben'd turn against me. Always sort've trusted him ... where're Cass and them others?'

'Up on the mountain.'

'Looking for you?'

'That's right, Pa. I came back to get you and Ben. He fooled me, too.'

Suddenly angry, Stoyers said: 'You've done enough yammering. Get back over here where I can keep an eye on you.'

Joel rose slowly and turned. The old cook

had changed his position. He now stood near the partly open door so he had the light to his back and could see the interior of the cabin better. Kane gave the situation a swift survey. If he could get within reaching distance of that door... Moving with deliberation, he crossed to the wall and leaned against it. Ignoring the stinging pain the pressure evoked in his shoulders, he folded his arms and stared at Stoyers.

'Can't figure you, Ben ... siding with Berryman. What'll you get out of it?'

'My share,' the old man said promptly. 'And I'll be my own boss. Won't be anybody walking in on me and chewing me out all the time.'

'Maybe. I can't see Cass taking you in, giving you any part of a split.'

'He will ... told me he would.'

'And you're fool enough to believe him? Hell, you're not as smart as I figured.'

'You don't know a thing about it!' Stoyers yelled, thoroughly aroused. 'I'll be getting...'

Joel kicked out like a striking rattlesnake.

His booted foot caught the forward panel of the door, which swung hard and slammed into Ben Stoyers. The rifle in Ben's hands exploded, sending the bullet into the floor. The weapon itself went flying into a corner of the room.

'Damn you...!' Stoyers yelled, and stumbled backward through the doorway.

Joel was across the room in a single bound, arms reaching for the rifle. Gathering it up, he levered a fresh cartridge into the chamber, whirling to peer through the layers of hanging smoke.

The half bent figure of the cook, Joel's pistol in his hand, was crouched just outside. Stoyers caught a glimpse of Kane and fired hurriedly – missed.

'Drop that gun!' Joel yelled, keeping the wall between him and the man. 'You haven't got a chance!'

'The hell I ain't!' Stoyers shouted back and, triggering the pistol again, lunged through the doorway.

Joel Kane fired once. The slug buried itself

in Stoyers's chest, halted his forward motion, and slammed him half around. He dropped his weapon and grabbed frantically for the door frame. For several seconds he clung to it, and then abruptly collapsed.

Kane bent hurriedly, scooped up his pistol, and wheeled to Amos. 'Got to pull out fast,' he said, tugging at the cord that bound the old man's wrists. 'Cass and the others are sure to have heard that shooting. Think you can ride?'

'Manage ... somehow,' Amos answered haltingly. 'Ben dead?'

Joel nodded. 'Tried to talk him out of it. He wouldn't listen.'

'He was a fool,' the old man said, struggling to his feet with Joel's aid. He leaned against the wall. 'Things are sort of fuzzy. Reckon it's that rap on the head Ben give me.'

'Soon as you're outside breathing some fresh air, you'll be all right.'

Throwing one arm around his father's slight body, Kane started for the door. They reached the opening, stepped over Ben

Stoyers's lifeless shape, and moved into the cool, silvered night.

'Horses ... they're right ahead, Pa,' Joel said. 'Keep resting on me. We'll make it.'

In that next moment Kane realized he and Amos were going nowhere – at least alone. Waiting at the edge of the shadows fronting the cabin was Cass Berryman. Strung out to either side, in a half circle, were Bill Taney, Clete Jordan, and the *vaquero*, Dobe Rivera.

Berryman said: 'Go ahead, friend. Load the old man on his horse.'

Joel hung motionless in the center of the clearing, Amos leaning heavily against him. A sullen anger was moving through him – not so much at the outlaws but at himself and his own carelessness. He should have used more care. He should've realized Berryman and his men would be near and prepared for them.

'Reckon you better get rid of that pistol first,' Bill Taney said.

Kane remained frozen, his mind reaching out, striving to find a means for meeting and overcoming this new emergency. Taney cocked his revolver, the distinct clicks loud in the stillness.

'Now!' he commanded harshly, leveling the weapon.

Joel drew the pistol with his free hand and allowed it to drop.

Berryman laughed. 'Put your pa on his horse, like I told you.'

Kane, supporting his father, walked to the side of the gray. Cradling the older man as he would a child, Joel lifted him onto the saddle. Amos groaned softly, sagged forward.

'Tie him,' Berryman said. 'Long ride ahead of us.'

Silent, tense with anger, Joel Kane lashed Amos to the saddle with a rope the outlaw tossed to him. That finished, he wheeled slowly. His pistol lay six feet away. The rifle was twice that distance, near the doorway of the cabin where he had dropped it. His chances for reaching either were less than none at all. He raised his eyes to the red-haired outlaw.

'Now what?'

Cass Berryman kneed his horse in closer. Extending his hand, he said: 'I'll take that paper you got at the bank.'

The will! Bitterness rolled through Joel. It was still in his pocket. He had planned to give it to Amos, let him have the satisfaction of destroying it. Now it was too late. He should have done it himself. 'What paper?' he asked coolly.

'Don't try bluffing me!' Berryman snapped. 'Raise your hands and keep them up.'

Kane lifted his arms. The outlaw leaned forward, probed Joel's pockets, and produced the document briefly, then nodded in satisfaction.

'Old Ben was right,' he said, and thrust the paper inside his shirt front. 'That god-damn' Testman's going to hear from me about this.' His glance paused on the body of the cook, half in and half out of the cabin's entrance. 'Get Stoyers's horse,' he said to Taney. 'Wouldn't be smart to leave him here.'

The outlaw spurred off into the brush.

Clete Jordan hawked, spat. 'You still figure

on taking them to Mud Lake?'

'That's my plan. Best and safest way to handle it.'

Joel forced a laugh. 'You'll have trouble explaining this.'

'Not me,' Cass Berryman said, folding his hands on the horn of his saddle. 'Your pa'll never be missed, and tramps like you come and go.'

'Little different with me. I was seen in town and folks know who I am. The marshal was one of them.'

'Eli Pryor? Expect I can handle him. I'll just give him and his missus a side of good beef and that'll end it.'

'Said there were others.'

'Testman? You mean him and his teller? No problem there, either. Henry knows what's good for him ... same as the teller. You're barking up the wrong tree, Kane. Made a big mistake trying to buck me.'

Bill Taney appeared at the edge of the clearing, a small buckskin in tow. He halted near the shack and dropped the leathers.

Berryman motioned to Joel. 'Hand Stoyers across the saddle. Better lash him down, too. Pick up the guns while you're there,' he added to Taney.

The husky outlaw came off his mount as Joel walked slowly to where Stoyers lay. Kane knew he had no choice but to do as he was told – for the time being, anyway. Later his chance might come.

Bill grinned at him as he scooped up the pistol and turned to retrieve the rifle. 'You ain't doing so good, mister.'

Joel said nothing. He knelt beside the crumpled body of the cook, lifting him easily, and draped him over the buckskin's saddle. Pulling the coil of rope free of the skirt, he tied the body securely into place. Stepping back, he collided with Taney, who was returning to his horse.

'Damn it ... watch what you're doing!' the outlaw yelled and struck out angrily.

The backhand slap landed on the side of Joel's head. It did no damage, but he recognized his opportunity, and seized it. 'Sure!' he answered, and drove his fist into the husky man's middle.

The blow was too high. Taney merely grunted, cursed again, and swung hard. Joel dodged and sent two more quick jabs into the man's face. Berryman shouted something, but Joel was too intent on drawing in Taney to hear. If he could maneuver the outlaw into the right position, he would not only have a shield but could gain possession of a weapon as well.

He pulled back, leading Taney on. The squat outlaw, face red, mouth working with a wild fury, rushed in. Joel, shoulders now to the wall of the cabin, set himself for a blow that'd stun the man, stop him cold. Taney lunged within reach. Kane started an uppercut from his heels, cleared the way for it with a sharp left jab to the outlaw's eyes. His knuckles cracked as his fist connected with Bill Taney's jaw. The husky rider halted as if he had walked into a stone wall. His arms fell to his sides, and he began to sway. Instantly Joel leaped forward, caught him around the waist with his left arm, and snatched the pistol from its holster with his right hand.

'Kane!'

Berryman's voice brought him up short. Revolver cocked, he looked across the clearing. His hopes died.

The outlaw chief had spurred in close to Amos. The *vaquero* had swung in also, was now on the opposite side of the old man. Both had their weapons out and were holding them against Amos Kane's bowed head.

'You want to see him die quick, try using that iron,' Cass Berryman said.

Joel straightened slowly. Sucking deep for lost breath, he released Taney, who staggered forward, still groggy.

'The gun,' Berryman pressed.

Joel tossed the weapon aside, felt a heaviness settle over him. It had almost worked – almost. Now...?

He was aware suddenly of Bill Taney wheeling, swinging a wild blow at his head. He heard the outlaw's enraged voice lashing him, cursing, threatening, as he tried to avoid the man's oncoming fist. Too late. He took a solid jolt to the ear. Lights popped before his eyes, his senses reeled, and he felt himself going down. Berryman was again yelling. His words seemed to come from a great distance.

He was on the ground, only half unconscious from the hard blow. He stirred. The sharp toe of a boot smashed cruelly into his ribs. Hands pulled at him, dragged him upright. He tried to stand, but there was no strength in his legs, and once more he started to sink.

'Hold him, damn it!' someone nearby shouted impatiently. 'I'll get his horse.'

Through the fog that blurred his vision, Joel made out the face of Clete Jordan. Taney was turning toward the sorrel, and, on beyond, Cass Berryman and the *vaquero* sat their saddles and watched in silence.

The sorrel was in front of him, crowding him. He felt himself being boosted, then dumped onto the saddle. Bill Taney's voice registered dully on his mind.

'We have to tie him, too?'

'Let him set a minute,' Berryman answered. 'He'll come out of it.'

'A wild one,' the ordinarily silent *vaquero* commented. 'In my country one we would say *muy macho*.'

'He ain't so much,' Taney said. 'Grabbed me when I was looking the other way.'

'Doesn't seem to make much difference whether you're looking or not,' Berryman said dryly. 'Now, keep away from him, hear? I don't want him making another try.'

'I'm not done with him ... not by a damn' sight!' the husky outlaw declared. 'Got me a few licks coming and I aim to get them.'

'You want us to hold him for you ... maybe tie his hands behind him?'

Joel, fully conscious, sat motionless with his head down while he listened. It wasn't over yet – not as long as he was still alive.

'Won't need any help!' Bill Taney roared. 'Turn me loose with him ... I'll show you.'

'Maybe. Anyway, you're not the only one wanting a piece of him. Clete figures he's got himself a claim, too.'

Jordan shrugged, turned to his horse. 'I'll collect ... but it'll be my way. I'm not fool enough to try using my fists ... not with him.'

'Well, I'm not scared of him!' Taney said. 'I don't need any hog-leg!'

'You need something,' Berryman said laconically. 'Shake him a mite, wake him up.'

The bearded outlaw whirled, grasped Joel by the arm, and jerked violently. Kane, hoping to maintain the deception further, mumbled thickly, sagged to one side.

'He can ride,' Berryman said. 'Mount up. I want to reach Mud Lake and get this job over with before daylight.'

X

They moved off downtrail. Dobe Rivera was in the lead. Behind him was Berryman, followed by Amos Kane, then Joel, Clete Jordan, Taney, and, last of all, the horse bearing the body of Stoyers. At the start Joel watched his father anxiously, not certain he was in condition to ride, but Amos, securely lashed to the saddle, appeared to be in fair shape although still somewhat dazed.

They descended slowly. Despite the brightness of the moon, shadows lay across the path, spooking the horses and causing them to proceed with caution. For this Joel Kane was grateful. It would take several hours to reach Mud Lake, and he needed every possible moment to find a way out for Amos and himself.

The posse? He thought of Eli Pryor and the men he had seen from the rimrocks, scouring the flats. Had they returned to Cedar River – or had the gunshots at the cabin drawn their attention? It was possible. Sound carried to great distances in the cold, clear air, and the old lawman and his party could, at that very moment, be working up the slope. But it could be no ace in the hole for him. Cass Berryman had spoken as if the marshal was something of a friend and would side with him after taking a bribe to look the other way. And from what he knew of Berryman, Joel had little reason to doubt his claim of influence.

He sighed heavily. There was little hope of help coming from anyone. Everything was stacked against him; it seemed foolish to buck such odds. But Joel Kane was not one to quit; as long as he had breath, he'd fight. Better to die from a bullet, anyway, than in the suffocating layers of slimy gumbo in Mud Lake. He glanced up. Amos, head sagged forward, rode the gray lifelessly, his frail body moving and shifting with the movements of his horse. Beyond him Berryman was a blocky outline in the night. Rivera, the silver trappings on his broad-brimmed Mexican hat glittering brightly, was a length farther away.

Joel ventured a look over his shoulder. Clete Jordan, both hands resting on the horn, face tipped down, rode wearily. He was not sleeping, Kane realized, but was in that nether world of tired half wakefulness. He brought his attention back around. Sheer wall lifted on his right, but to the left a slope fell away, steeply in some places, more gradual in others, and all thickly brushed. A man could break at the proper moment, send his horse plunging into the undergrowth, and possibly make good an escape. It wasn't for him. Cass Berryman knew he would not make such an effort, was so certain of it, in fact, that he had foregone binding Joel's wrists. The outlaw had Amos, and, as long as he did, he knew he held the upper hand.

Joel had to think of something else – something that would provide escape for both Amos and himself. He shook his head wearily. It was a big order, one that would be difficult to fill. The trail began to level off, and Joel realized they were moving onto the flats that stretched out from the base of the mountains. He glanced around once more, growing more desperate for some means of escape. Jordan stirred into life, and Taney, taking note for the first time, gave him a hard-cornered grin.

'Something bothering you, saddlebum?'

Instantly Cass Berryman turned on his saddle. 'Shut up back there,' he hissed. 'I don't want any racket.'

The meaning of that drove home to Kane. The outlaw leader had also seen the posse and was hoping to avoid it. Apparently Cass wasn't as sure of Eli Pryor as he had claimed. Or perhaps it was the men riding with the marshal. They would be local citizens of Cedar River, and probably not ones to be intimidated by the red-headed outlaw. Hope began to stir again within Joel.

Abruptly the horse ahead of him stopped. Joel looked up quickly. Berryman, hand raised, was in the center of the trail. Rivera had pulled off to the side and was staring into the brush.

'What's the trouble?' Taney's question was a hoarse whisper.

'That posse we saw, probably,' Clete Jordan murmured.

At that moment the *vaquero* wheeled, doubled back to where Berryman waited.

He spoke a few quick words to the outlaw. Berryman immediately raised himself in his stirrups and made a quick survey. Obviously he was seeking a place in which to hide.

Again Cass Berryman lifted his arm, this time waving the party off the trail and pointing to a thick stand of juniper and other growth. Rivera spurred off the path, catching the reins of Amos's gray as he crossed. Berryman swung in behind them, and at the same instant Clete crowded by Joel, forcing the sorrel to turn, head into the trees.

'Try something and I'll split your head open,' Bill Taney warned, brandishing his pistol as he cut in beside Joel. 'Hear?'

Joel nodded. It was not yet time to make a move, if one was to be made. Best wait until the marshal and his men were near and there was no doubt of their passing by. It could be they were only in the area, and Cass Berryman was just playing it safe.

Silent, he lined up with the others in the deep shadows, aware that Clete Jordan had taken up a position slightly to his rear, Taney farther over. The moments dragged. Far off in the distance an owl hooted. A hoof clicked sharply against a rock. Again there was quiet – and then a horse and rider appeared at a bend in the trail. A second moved into view, then a third. Joel strained to make out the first man's identity. Moonlight glinted against metal on his vest. Relief sped through Kane: Eli Pryor, the marshal. It was the posse. Joel tensed, but allowed the seconds to tick by, waited until the lawman was directly opposite.

'Marshal!' he called in a clear voice, and started to spur into the open.

Pryor halted, and instantly Jordan jammed his pistol into Kane's back, murmured: 'Sit tight. Take a look at the Mex.'

Joel froze and swung his eyes to the *vaquero*. Rivera had his knife out, was pressing the point against the elder Kane's throat.

'Who's there?' Pryor asked, staring into the black depths of the junipers.

Cass Berryman moved onto the shoulder of the trail. 'Evening, Marshal,' he said easily.

The lawman glared at him. 'What the hell do you mean, scaring a man like that?'

Berryman laughed. 'Sorry, Eli. Didn't mean to.'

The old lawman settled back, still frowning. 'You hiding from somebody?'

'Reckon you could say that. Heard you coming ... weren't sure who it'd be. Pulled off into the brush until we had a look. Lot of owlhoot running loose around here these days.'

'So I been told,' Pryor said dryly. 'Little late to be riding the hills, ain't it?'

The marshal didn't appear to be much of a friend to Berryman, Joel thought, and wondered if he dared trust the man. Regardless, he couldn't be much worse off.

The outlaw leader said: 'Heard shooting up in the rimrocks. Some of the boys and I rode up to see what it was all about.'

Pryor shifted wearily. 'Find out?'

'Sure did. Guess it's a job for you, Marshal. Somebody killed my cook.'

The lawman came to attention. 'Stoyers?

Thought he worked for old man Kane.'

'Same thing,' Berryman said with a wave of his hand, 'seeing as how I'm running the place for Kane.'

Pryor digested that, said: 'Who did it?'

'Don't know. Whoever it was had lit out. We picked up some tracks heading west. Lost them in the dark.'

Surprise stirred Joel. He had half expected the outlaw to name him as the killer – it would have been a simple way for Berryman to rid himself of a problem. But the redhead evidently believed it safer to handle the matter in a different manner. Joel leaned forward. If he could draw Pryor's attention, get recognized... Jordan's gun barrel dug deeper into his spine. 'You forgetting the Mex?' the gunman muttered.

Joel relaxed. Pryor drew a pipe from his pocket, tamped it full of tobacco. Striking a match, he puffed for several moments, then returned his attention to Cass.

'You leave Stoyers's body up there?'

'Having the boys bring it down. Aim to

give the old man a decent burial. Sure hope you can catch that killer, Eli. Ben never harmed anybody.'

'I'll get him,' the lawman said, looking up the trail. 'Whereabouts did it happen?'

'That old cabin, south end of the rimrocks.'

Pryor twisted around and nodded to the men gathered into a group behind him. 'Let's get up there, boys. We'll camp till daylight, then start doing some tracking.'

'Smart idea, Marshal,' Berryman said, shaking his head admiringly. 'Killer's probably holed up for the night, and you being there at daylight'll give you a good start. Need any help?'

'Reckon I got enough,' the lawman said. 'Obliged just the same.'

'Just offering to do my part,' the outlaw said smoothly. 'My place and my men ... they're available to you any time you say the word.'

'Obliged,' Eli Pryor said again and, motioning to the riders behind him, started up the trail.

Cass Berryman wheeled around and rode

up to Joel. His eyes were narrow and his face was set in grim lines. 'Thought you'd pull a smart one, eh!' he snarled, and struck Joel hard across the mouth.

Joel recoiled, tasting the warm salt of blood from his lips. He stared at the outlaw, his own anger a steady, simmering hate. Another chance for escape had failed – and now he was grasping at straws. Berryman was riled plenty. If he could incense him further, cause him to make a false move, create an opening – shrugging, Kane forced a grin. 'Remembered you talking about the marshal. Just trying to see if you were the big man you claimed.'

'Don't worry about him. He'll do what I tell him.'

'Not worrying about anything. I figure that posse'll be back. They didn't swallow that yarn you handed them.'

The red-haired outlaw glanced at Clete Jordan, betraying for the first time a thread of uncertainty. It was only a fleeting expression, however. He laughed. 'That's what you're hoping.'

'Easy to see,' Joel said. 'Pryor knows me, heard what I told the banker about you ... and what you're doing to my pa. Trying to pass Stoyers off as one of your bunch was a bad mistake.'

Berryman considered that in silence. Joel watched the man closely, searching for signs of his weakening. He had no actual belief in the words he had spoken – doubted if Eli Pryor had even registered the slip about who Stoyers had worked for, but he had to push every possible opportunity, work any and all angles.

Bill Taney spurred up to Berryman's side. 'Aw, he's just talking, Cass,' he said. 'They didn't figure anything was wrong.'

'Believing that,' Joel said, pressing hard, 'will be another mistake. Face it, Berryman. Your string's run out. Better turn Pa and me loose and make a run for it while you've still got a chance.'

Berryman raised his head and brushed back his hat. 'Not much, I won't,' he said, coming to a decision. 'The marshal couldn't prove anything, no matter what he might think. And with you and the old man gone ... lying under twenty feet of mud...'

'Ought to be moving out of here,' Jordan broke in, looking uptrail, 'just in case that posse does take a notion to come back.'

Berryman nodded. 'Expect you're right. The sooner we get them out of the way, the easier it'll be to handle things.' He swung to Taney. 'Bill, take Stoyers's body and head for the ranch. I want you to stay there and wait.'

'Now wait a minute,' the bearded outlaw began. 'I'm not...'

'Stay there,' Berryman repeated in a flat voice. 'If Pryor does show up, I want him thinking things are just the way I said.'

'He'll be looking for you. Where'll I say you are?'

'In town. Went there to make arrangements for burying Stoyers. I don't think you'll have any problems. There's a chance we'll be back before they show up ... if they do.'

Taney swore. 'Why can't Jordan do it ... or

Dobe? Why's it have to be me?'

'Because I'm telling you to,' Berryman snapped, and pulled away. 'All right, let's move out.'

'You heard him,' Jordan said, and prodded Joel roughly with his pistol.

Joel, disappointment and frustration again weighting him heavily, put the sorrel into motion, swung in behind Amos. The older man appeared to have recovered somewhat and now seemed aware of what was taking place. He glanced at Joel, smiled wryly, apologetically. Joel nodded faintly, wishing he could convey some reassurance to him.

As before, Rivera led the party. He rode a short distance ahead, continually on the alert as if afraid of encountering others. That seemed unlikely to Joel. At that hour of the night he could scarcely expect anyone to be abroad, especially since they were on Circle K land. One thing he had learned. Berryman was not the all-powerful man he sought to make others believe, and again Joel began to search his mind for a way to tear at the outlaw's self-assurance, create doubts, and provide an opening. One thing was good – with Bill Taney gone he had only three to contend with.

They rode on through the night, crossing the ranch at a long diagonal that would take them from the extreme southwest corner to a point just beyond the northeast boundary. But Joel Kane had no time for interest in his surroundings or the beauty of the warm, silver-lighted darkness. With each passing mile they were drawing closer to Mud Lake – and the end for Amos and himself.

He wondered if Eli Pryor had been suspicious, as he had tried to make Berryman believe. If so, the old lawman had played it cool, making it appear he was going along with what the outlaw had told him. But if that were true, why hadn't he and his posse reappeared? Could it be he was trailing Berryman's party at a safe distance, waiting to see what the outlaw intended to do? Did Cass Berryman also have such thoughts? – he was keeping Dobe Rivera ranging wide, maintaining a sharp lookout.

He couldn't rely on such a frail possibility, Joel knew. There was a chance it was true – but only a chance. Deep within him another conviction relative to the old lawman had begun to form, and grow in strength: Eli Pryor, like so many small-town marshals, was nothing more than a badge – a hollow representative of the law, useful only in serving legal papers and jailing Saturday night drunks.

Joel glanced over his shoulder. Jordan was immediately behind him, watching him with a quiet, deadly intensity. He wished Berryman had sent Clete back with the cook's body and left Bill Taney to guard him. Taney was the sort who could be tricked, and the possibility of escape would have been much greater. Likely Cass Berryman realized that and had chosen Jordan intentionally, thus ridding himself of Taney and potential trouble.

Joel looked again to his father. The old man rode head bowed and slumped in the saddle, but he was no longer limp. Undoubtedly he felt much better – but he would still be of little use in a showdown of any sort. Amos's legs were lashed together, holding him firmly to his horse. But even if he rode free, he could be of small help. Anything that was to be done, Joel guessed, he'd have to do alone.

A long ridge, dark against the star-littered sky, began to take shape ahead. Kane's nerves tightened as he realized its meaning. Beyond it lay the swale in which was pocketed Mud Lake. Tension began to lay its hard pressure upon him – time was running out. Once more he turned to Clete Jordan. The gunman's gaze was unwavering, and he now rode with one hand resting on the butt of his pistol.

A thought entered Joel Kane's mind. Why hadn't the outlaws used bullets on Amos and him? Why hadn't they simply killed them back at the cabin, or somewhere along the trail, taken their bodies to Mud Lake, and tossed them into the slime? Why was Berryman doing it the hard way? It wasn't that the outlaw chief wished to avoid the sound of gunshots. There had been plenty of those racketing across the slopes and flats. Could it be that Berryman, in his almost fanatical desire to keep everything legal, wished to avoid direct murder and sought to make his and Amos's death appear accidental? It was splitting a hair pretty fine, but Cass was of that turn of mind. He could stand and in truth swear under oath that neither he nor any of his men ever used a weapon of any sort on the Kanes – and to his way of thinking his conscience would be clear.

It didn't really matter, Joel realized. When a man was dead, he was dead regardless of how it came to pass. But the thought did offer a glimmer of hope, a thin one to be sure, but at this point Joel Kane was ready to try anything.

Up ahead, Dobe Rivera had halted. Berryman moved in beside him, and both were looking down at the far side of the slope. Joel didn't need to be told what they saw – Mud Lake.

XI

Jordan said: 'Get on up there with the others.'

Joel touched the sorrel lightly with his spurs, guided him to the top of the ridge. Halting beside Amos, he looked down into the swale. The bog, its thick, oily surface gleaming dully in the moonlight, appeared to have shrunk, and he wondered if it could be gradually drying up. If and when that day came, it would be a blessing. Much good beef had been lost in its choking depths – and who could say for certain there had been no human victims?

'You still set against using a gun?' Jordan asked.

Berryman nodded. 'Do it like I said, just in case.'

'It's not going to be easy.'

'Why not? Just stampede the horses down

the slope. It's dark enough ... they'll run right into the mud. Better cut the old man loose.'

Clete did not move. 'What about tracks?'

'Drag some brush. That'll wipe all the sign out.'

Joel cast a covert glance at Jordan. The gunman was no longer directly behind him, and Jordan's hand was clear of the weapon at his side. Joel looked then to Amos, found his father staring at him intently. The old man raised his hands slightly, flipped his eyes. Joel looked more closely. The lead rope held by Berryman was no longer tied to the gray horse. Amos had worked the knot apart and now held the two ends to make it appear the rope was secure.

The younger Kane grinned and made a swift appraisal. The ridge, where they had halted, was barren except for small clumps of snakeweed. Farther back down the slope, however, there were considerable brush and a few cedars. Joel jerked his head in that direction, endeavoring to make Amos understand that he should follow that route if the opportunity came. The older man moved his lips soundlessly. Joel hoped it was an indication that he had gotten the message.

'What's wrong with right here?' Jordan asked. 'Slope's plenty steep.'

'More rocks on the far side, be less tracks to worry about,' Cass Berryman explained.

Jordan shrugged. 'Well, let's get at it.'

Joel Kane realized he would never have a better chance to make his try. He had only a faint hope of success, anyway, but it was not in him to submit meekly to death.

'Go, Pa!' he yelled, and drove his spurs deep into the sorrel's flanks.

Startled, the big red plunged forward, straight into Clete Jordan's mount. As they came together, Joel struck out with his balled fist, smashed a shocking blow into the gunman's face.

Clete yelled as he went off the saddle backward, clawing at the hull to save himself. Instantly Joel was off the sorrel and upon the outlaw, wrenching the man's weapon from its holster.

To his left he saw Amos whirling away on the gray, dragging Berryman with him. The outlaw leader had apparently wrapped the lead rope about his wrist and was unable to free himself quickly enough to avoid being jerked off his horse. But it was only temporary. He shook loose and struggled to regain his feet. Joel, vaulting back onto the sorrel, saw Berryman draw his weapon and take hurried aim at Amos, racing down the slope. Again cruelly spurring the sorrel, Joel drove straight at the outlaw chief.

Dobe Rivera yelled a warning, and Berryman paused, threw himself from the path of the red, and tried to swing around for a shot at Joel. Joel fired hastily, spoiling Berryman's try – and then snapped a shot at the *vaquero,* who was crouched and leveling his pistol with both hands.

Rivera jolted as Kane's bullet struck him, began to stagger. Berryman was down – not hit, Joel was sure – but entangled in his own feet. He flung a glance to the slope. Amos and the gray had reached the comparative safety of the brush. He... Joel felt arms grip him from behind. Clete Jordan! He had forgotten the gunman. The outlaw's hands were dragging at him, striving to pull him from the sorrel, now wheeling to head down the slope. Berryman was shouting, and beyond him the Mexican was a folded shape in the moonlight.

Kane, holding tightly to Jordan's pistol, struggled to rip the man's fingers away with his free hand. He locked about one wrist and tore at it savagely, but he could not break the outlaw's grip. The sorrel, frantic now from the weight dragging at his side, began to plunge and dance nervously.

'Get away from him ... get away!'

It was Berryman, shouting at Jordan. The redhead was standing near Rivera, pistol raised, attempting to get a clean shot. Joel hammered at Jordan's head and neck, glanced down the slope. Amos had halted and was waiting.

'Go on! The ranch!' he yelled. 'I'll catch up!'

The elder Kane slapped at the gray's rump and moved off at a trot. With his feet still bound together Amos was having a hard time of it.

Joel turned his attention again to Clete Jordan. The man was hanging onto him like a leech, and it seemed impossible to jar him loose. He looked then to Berryman. The outlaw leader had forsaken Rivera and was running toward his horse a few yards away. Kane raised his weapon, snapped a shot at the man.

The outlaw halted abruptly, and dropped to one knee. His pistol blasted a small orange spot in the silver night, and Joel saw sand spurt up immediately in front of the sorrel. Berryman would hold back no longer, Jordan or not, Joel realized.

Twisting, he renewed his efforts to knock Clete loose. Using the pistol as a club, he struck at the man's locked hands. Jordan's fingers parted, and he slipped a few inches. Joel struck again, at the gunman's head this time. The blow landed on Jordan's neck.

Clete yelled and grabbed for the weapon, at the same time releasing his grasp of Joel.

Kane felt the pistol tear from his fingers as Jordan fell away and went sprawling onto the sand. The sorrel, clear of the maddening, encumbering weight, whirled and rushed off.

Joel started to pull up, to return to where Jordan lay stunned, and recover the revolver. The sharp crack of Berryman's pistol changed his thought. Bending low, he raked the big red with his rowels and plunged downgrade in pursuit of Amos.

He overtook the older man a short mile later.

Amos greeted him anxiously. 'You hurt?'

Kane shook his head. 'Got to keep moving. They're coming after us.'

'Heard shooting. Thought maybe you needed help.'

'Downed the Mexican. Lost the gun, fighting with Jordan. Too late to go back for it.'

He turned and stared over his shoulder. There was no sign of Berryman and Clete Jordan – but they wouldn't lose any time.

One thing, he thought grimly, there'd be only the two of them. The odds were better.

'We heading for the ranch?' Amos yelled to be heard above the thud of the horses' hoofs.

'Best place. Too far to town ... never get there.'

'Can't do much good at the ranch.'

'We can fort up, hold out until Pryor and that posse get there.'

'If they get there. You forgetting Bill Taney's waiting ... maybe some of the others?'

Joel shook his head. 'Haven't forgotten. We'll just get around him somehow.'

They rushed on through the night. It was easy going for the horses, most of it downgrade, and even the gray was taking it with no difficulty.

From time to time Joel looked back, and finally he saw two riders silhouetted briefly on a hillock. Cass Berryman and Jordan were moving up – fast. To hold their lead, the sorrel and the gray needed to increase their pace. He glanced at the gray. The horse was doing his best. Kane swore, resigned himself to luck. They could make it, but it would be close.

He swung the sorrel in closer to Amos. The older man's face was stiff with pain. The punishment he was taking was evident, and Joel knew they should stop and cut his legs free, but it would mean nothing less than suicide. He drew his father's attention.

'Who else are we liable to find at the ranch?'

'The two you saw at the barn. Maybe a couple of others who've been out, scouting up stock.'

'They sleep in the house?'

'Got a place off the side of the barn. Little shack.' Amos paused, then: 'You were saying something about the marshal. You figuring on him for help?'

Joel checked the back trail again. At first he saw nothing, and worry instantly sprang alive within him. Had the outlaws cut off, taken a shorter route that would bring them in ahead? He couldn't recall any other road, but he'd been away ten long years, and things change ... in the next moment he saw them, and relief eased his nerves. They had just been in a low spot, out of view. They had gained, but it couldn't be helped.

'I said ... the marshal. You depending on him for help?'

Amos yelled his question a second time. Joel shook his head. 'Hoping ... but not depending. Expect it'll be up to you and me, Pa.'

Amos bobbed approvingly. 'Suits me. I reckon we can handle it.'

As they drew nearer to the ranch, Joel began to have second thoughts about his father and the wisdom of his being on hand when matters came to a head. Amos was in poor condition to face any sort of desperate situation, and it was doubtful he could be of any help. But Joel said nothing until they reached the far side of the house and quietly walked the horses up to the window where he had earlier entered the structure. There Joel swung down quickly, wheeled to Amos and, after pulling the rope free of the older man's ankles, faced him.

'Pa, I was thinking. It might be better for you to ride on into town. I'll hold Berryman and his bunch here. You won't run into trouble.'

Amos looked down at his son. 'That means you plain don't want me around?'

'Not that at all. Figured you'd be better off.'

Amos Kane shook his head. 'Be better off right here with my own kin, helping fight for what's ours. And if I don't come out of it with a whole skin, I'll leastways know I did what I could.'

Joel reached up, helped the older man to dismount. 'Whatever you say, Pa,' he replied, pride stirring him deeply. 'We'll give them one hell of a run for it.'

Leaning over, he quickly removed his spurs, hung them on the saddle horn, then pointed to the window. 'I crawled through there this morning. Cross over and wait while I have a look at the yard.'

'Berryman and Clete can't be far off,' Amos said. 'Keep your eyes peeled.'

Joel moved off at once, hurried along the side of the house. He knew he was cutting it thin. The two outlaws would be showing up any minute, but he had to get an idea of what he'd be up against once inside the building.

Reaching the corner, he halted. Two horses stood at the corral. The body of Ben Stoyers was on one; the other belonged to Bill Taney. Kane edged a few steps deeper into the yard, trying for a better look at the far end of the house. Light showed in the window – the kitchen – and he thought he could hear voices. Taney was not alone, apparently – but who could be with him? There were no other horses.

The hostlers? The answer came to him abruptly, and, pivoting, he retraced his steps to where Amos waited. Without hesitating, he boosted himself up, started through the window. One leg inside, he paused to look at Amos.

'There a gun somewhere in one of the back rooms?' he asked in a low whisper.

The elder Kane shook his head. 'Cass took them all. Afraid I might get ideas, I reckon.' He checked his words, added as an after-thought: 'Ben had an odd shotgun he used to hunt rabbit and quail with. Kept it in the kitchen.'

Joel remembered the shotgun. Likely it was still around as Stoyers had been carrying a rifle at the cabin. But if it was in the kitchen? – he shook his head as he climbed on through the window. Nothing ever came easy.

Hesitating briefly to listen and assure himself Taney had not been disturbed, he leaned forward and assisted Amos to enter. Cautioning the older man for silence, he pointed down the hallway.

'Taney's in there,' he murmured. 'Somebody's with him. Maybe those two hostlers ... couldn't tell for sure.'

'Probably right,' Amos said. 'They won't be packing guns. Bill Taney will. How...?'

'Got to surprise him. It's the only thing we can do, and we have to do it before Berryman and Jordan show up.'

'They ought to be showing up soon. What do you want me doing?'

'Stay behind me,' Joel said, and crossed to the hallway. Keeping close to the wall, he made his way toward the kitchen, halted just beside the doorway.

Bill Taney sat at the table, one leg thrown over a chair. He partly faced Joel and was talking to one of the hostlers, hunched against the wall to his left. There was no sign of the other stableman.

Taney would be hard to take by surprise. At the angle he faced he would see anyone in the hallway the moment of his appearance. Kane drew back to think, caught the faint sound of horses entering the yard. Cass Berryman and Jordan had arrived.

'That'll be Cass and the boys,' Taney said, dropping his foot to the floor.

The hostler raised himself, peered through the dust-streaked window. 'Only see two horses.'

The bearded outlaw lurched to his feet. 'Two?'

Crouched in the short hallway, Joel Kane prepared to lunge. He couldn't afford to let Bill Taney go out into the yard – he needed the outlaw's pistol. It would be easy to remain quiet, allow the bearded outlaw and the hostler to leave the house, and then take possession. But retaining possession without a weapon with which to fight was out of the question.

'That's all,' the hostler said, moving toward the door. 'Looks like Cass and Jordan ... sure don't see anything of the Mex.'

'Been trouble,' Taney said, and started across the room.

Joel hit the outlaw low and hard. The man yelled and tried to turn, but the force of Kane's rush carried him to the wall, sending a shower of cans and dishes clattering to the floor. The hostler, face white, took a single glance at the sudden eruption of confusion, and bolted into the yard, shouting for Berryman.

Joel heard only vaguely. The impact had jarred him, knocked him off balance. On hands and knees, he struggled to regain his footing, to seize Bill Taney before he could also recover and draw his weapon.

Joel grappled blindly. He caught the outlaw by an arm and jerked savagely. Taney, also on his knees, lashed out at Kane's face. Joel took the blow across the bridge of the nose and recoiled with pain. Taney shouted, then threw himself forward. Joel pulled aside quickly, chopping at the bearded man's neck with the heel of his hand. Bill sagged and clawed weakly for the pistol on his hip. Kane struck him again, and the weapon, half out of its holster, fell to the floor. Joel made a grab for it, but missed as Taney kneed him brutally in the belly.

He rolled to his back and slapped Taney smartly across the eyes. The outlaw cursed. He tried again to reach his pistol. Kane, striving to get his legs beneath him for the sake of leverage, hit him once more across the face. Bill grunted, but continued to claw at the revolver. Joel, sucking deep for wind, heaved himself half around and kicked. His foot struck the pistol and sent it skittering across the floor and under the table. Taney roared, jerked himself upright. He made a lunge to recover the weapon but tripped as Amos Kane shoved a chair into his path.

The outlaw went down. Joel was upon him instantly. He had to end the fight and do so quickly. Berryman and Clete Jordan would be closing in. He flung a glance at Amos. 'The lamp ... put it out!' he yelled, and swung hard at Taney.

The outlaw jerked away, took the blow on his shoulder. Twisting, he wrapped his arms about Joel's legs. Abruptly the room plunged into darkness as the elder Kane reached the wall lamp and twisted its wick.

Joel, laboring to keep his balance, hammered at Taney's neck and head. He felt the grip around his legs slacken, so he put more strength into his efforts. Suddenly he felt himself falling, going over backward. He tried to catch himself, failed, went down solidly, his right shoulder striking the edge of a chair, capsizing it. Instantly he rolled away, avoiding Taney's groping hands. He came up against another chair and tried to brush it aside, but it was wedged against the wall. Outside, Cass Berryman was yelling something. He sounded near – too near.

Heaving with all his strength, Kane lurched upright. Taney was a dark shape in the meager light supplied by the moon. Joel rushed in low, arm cocked. He drove a solid right into the outlaw's middle, jabbed a stinging left into his face. Taney groaned, spun about, staggered across the room and caught himself against the door frame. He hung there for a brief instant, then plunged out into the yard.

Gasping, Joel reached for the door, slammed it shut. Instantly guns began to crackle, and a dozen bullets ripped through the wooden panel.

XII

'Down!' Joel yelled, and threw himself to the floor.

Through the dust haze he saw Amos sprawl out near the table. Another blast of gunfire rocked the night and glass shattered as the window was blown into fragments.

'Pa ... you all right?'

Amos Kane's voice was low, taut. 'Those thieving, back-stabbing bastards ... shooting up a man's place like this!'

Joel grinned. It was the first time he could recall hearing his father speak in anger. It sounded good. Staying flat, he crawled to where Taney's pistol had slid, groped about until he located it. He felt better, then. Working his way to the center of the room, he said: 'We've got one gun between us. Need another one bad. Any idea where Stoyers kept

158

that scatter-gun?'

Amos was quiet for a few moments. 'Seems I recollect seeing him put it in that closet over near the door.'

'Kane!' Cass Berryman's voice sliced through the old man's words. 'You hear me, Kane?'

'Take a look,' Joel said, 'but keep down.'

Amos began to pull himself across the room, his boots making loud, scraping sounds against the floor.

'Kane ... you alive in there?'

'Try coming in and you'll find out!' Joel yelled.

A single gunshot followed. The bullet, coming through the empty window, struck high on the wall, dislodged the picture hanging there, and sent it crashing down. Amos swore deeply from his side of the room.

'Just letting you know we've got you penned up in there,' Cass Berryman called. 'Ain't a Chinaman's chance of you coming out alive.'

'Found it,' Amos Kane said in the half

dark. 'It was right where I figured ... in the closet.'

'Any shells?' Joel asked anxiously.

'Five ... couple in the barrels.'

Disappointment shook Joel. 'Help some,' he muttered.

'Scatter-gun's a mighty good weapon,' Amos said. 'Seen a man hold off a whole crowd with one.'

Kane agreed. Nobody liked to face a charge of buckshot, but the weapon's range was limited and with only seven loads...?

'Giving you a chance to come out of there!' Berryman yelled. 'Both of you ... walk out with your hands empty ... and up. You can keep right on going.'

'Get over to where you can watch the hallway,' Joel said quietly. 'One of them could try sneaking in through that window. I'll keep an eye on the yard.'

Amos hitched his way to where he could see down the corridor. Joel crawled closer to the window, raised his head carefully, and looked out into the yard. Berryman, flanked by Jordan and Bill Taney, was standing behind the corral, only partially visible. At the barn the two hostlers crouched in the doorway.

'Kane, you hear me?'

'I hear you,' Joel answered. 'We'll take our chances inside.'

'You're a fool. We can keep you pinned down till you starve.'

'Plenty of grub in here.'

'Be no trouble burning you out.'

'Don't figure you ought to try. First man that tries getting close is dead.'

'You can't be all over the place at one time. I've got enough help to get somebody through.'

'Sure ... just pick out the man who wants to die first. Let him start.'

Berryman was right. Joel and Amos could not cover every point, and, to make it worse, the north side was windowless and therefore blind. If the outlaws remembered that...

'What do you think?' Amos said. 'You figure we'd be smart to crawl back out that window, make a stand in the brush?'

Joel shook his head. 'They'd have us cold turkey then. Our best bet's here, inside.'

'Going to be hard, keeping them away from the house, if they take a notion to go circling around.'

'I can see all three of them. Both the hostlers, too. Any one of them starts across the yard, I'll nail him quick.'

'Kane, you coming out?' Berryman's tone was impatient. 'I don't aim to wait here all night.'

'Up to you,' Joel yelled. 'Best thing you can do is to take your bunch and ride on. You're not taking over this ranch.'

'I already have,' the outlaw answered.

Immediately guns opened up. Bullets thudded into the wall, smashed through the door. Kane, risking a hurried glance, saw a dark shadow pull away from the corral and, bending low, start for the far side of the house. Resting his pistol on the windowsill, he pressed off a shot at the hunched shape.

The bullet dug sand at the outlaw's feet,

brought him to a halt. Joel triggered a second shot, then ducked beneath the opening as Berryman and the man still beside him began to shoot.

Waiting until the firing had stopped, he again peered from a corner of the window. There were three figures at the corral again, two at the barn. Whoever it was that had taken it in mind to cross over had turned back. Hurriedly, Joel flipped open the loading gate of the pistol, punched out the spent cartridges. Thumbing two fresh shells from his belt, he tried to reload, then swore harshly. Taney's revolver was of a different caliber. His cartridges would not fit.

'Something wrong?' Amos asked.

'This gun ... my shells won't work. Got three shots left.'

The elder Kane groaned. 'Sure doesn't put us in such good shape,' he commented. 'There's no reason for your being in a mess like this. I was wrong in sending for you.'

'Forget it.'

'No, I'm not forgetting it. Not much hope

of us coming out of this alive, so I'm telling you I want you to crawl out that back window and...'

'No use talking that way, Pa.'

'Yes there is ... and it makes sense. It's not right that you should throw your life away on something you don't care a rap about. Let Berryman have the place ... I'm too old to give a damn.'

'Maybe I do care about it.'

Amos was silent. Finally he asked: 'You mean that? You're saying you aren't here just because you feel you have to be?'

'Just what I'm saying. Ranch is yours ... ours. Nobody's just going to up and take it away from us ... not without a fight, anyway. Thought we'd settled all this before.'

Joel paused, looked again through the window. He frowned. He could see only two dark shapes in the shadows behind the corral. Worry began to tag him, and, ducking low, he moved to the opposite side of the window for a better view. One outlaw was missing.

'Watch that hallway,' he warned. 'They're

up to something.'

'I'm watching,' Amos replied, and shifted his position to one nearer the door.

Joel resumed his post at the window, kept his eyes searching the yard and the brush along its edge, alert for any movement that would betray the location of the outlaw. The hostlers, he noted, were still in the doorway of the barn.

A horse stamped wearily. The sound came from the north side of the house. It caused Joel's thoughts to swing to Eli Pryor and the posse, somewhere up on the mountain. Would they hear the gunshots and hurry down to investigate? And where would the lawman stand – with Cass Berryman? He wished he knew how to figure the marshal. If he could be sure of a fair deal from him, there would be good reason to hold out against the outlaws until the posse could arrive. But Pryor was an unknown factor. His presence could make matters worse. And their position was bad – Joel was not fooling himself for one instant about that.

With a revolver containing three bullets and a shotgun that was of little use except in close quarters, he couldn't put up much of a fight. Berryman held all the cards despite the fact he was outside the house. The house, Kane thought grimly, could become a deathtrap instead of a fortress.

The room rocked suddenly with the deafening blast of the shotgun. Amos yelled, and Joel, wheeling about, saw him stiffen, then drop the long-barreled weapon. The hallway was boiling with smoke, and back in its depths there was a crumpled, smoldering heap.

'Pa!' Joel shouted and, forgetting caution, leaped across the room.

Amos Kane lay on his back. A deep stain was spreading slowly down his right chest. The old man grinned. 'Ain't bad,' he muttered. 'I ... I get him?'

Joel squinted again into the corridor. The haze had lifted somewhat, and he saw Clete Jordan. The charge from the shotgun had caught him straight on, done terrible things to him.

'You got him,' Joel said. He rose partly and glanced out the window. Berryman and Taney were still near the corral, unaware, of course, as to how Jordan had fared. He turned back to Amos, made a quick examination of the older man's wound. It was high, just below the shoulder, and ordinarily would not be too serious. But Amos could stand to lose little blood, and at his age the shock was almost as lethal as a bullet. He would need medical attention – and very soon.

'Kane!' Berryman's voice was loud. 'That's only the start...!'

Anger roared through Joel in a gusty blast. He spun to the window. 'You're right ... only the start! Jordan's dead ... and it's your turn now!'

Bending down, he snatched up the shotgun, replaced the spent shell, and, thrusting the pistol into his holster, whirled to the door. Joel lunged through the opening, burst into the yard. Not slowing his steps, he aimed the shotgun from the hip, fired the left barrel at the two men crouched near the corral, then rushed on.

A yell went up, and instantly pistol shots began to fill the pale night. Bullets plucked at Kane's weaving shape, spouted sand and dust over his feet. He reached the center of the yard. Berryman was now in view, away from the protection of the corral poles.

Swinging the shotgun around, Joel released the second charge. Berryman screamed, slammed up against the corner of the pen. Joel dropped the now useless long gun and reached for the pistol. Beyond Berryman's body he could see Bill Taney, moving forward. Bill had held back, allowing Cass to take the shotgun's blast. Now, certain Kane was unarmed and helpless, he was closing in for the kill.

Joel halted abruptly, brought up his pistol, and fired. He felt a powerful force slap solidly against him, spin him half around. He knew he had been hit. Taney and he had triggered their weapons at the identical instant.

Unaccountably he was on one knee. Twisting, he aimed again at the bearded Taney, but the outlaw was sinking, pitching forward. Joel swung his attention to the barn. The two hostlers raised their arms hurriedly.

'Don't shoot! We're not armed!' one yelled in a frantic voice.

Joel waved the pistol at them. 'Get a team and wagon over here! Got to get my pa to the doctor!'

One of the pair dodged back into the darkness of the barn immediately. The other turned to follow, then halted. There was a quick rush of hoofs as horsemen swept into the yard. Pryor and the posse.

Joel, battling a haziness that was creeping over him, pulled himself upright, faced the approaching lawman warily. Pryor walked his horse in close, his glance sweeping the scene, touching the sprawled Taney and, farther over, Cass Berryman.

'Some of you take a look at those two,' he called over his shoulder, and then settled his hard gaze on Joel. 'What the hell's going on here?'

'You're a little late,' Joel said coldly, and turned to the barn where the second hostler still stood in the doorway. 'God damn it, get that wagon over here!'

The man disappeared into the structure. Pryor leaned forward in his saddle. 'You haven't answered my question, mister.'

'Both the others are dead ... Cass Berryman and Bill Taney,' one of the posse members said, stepping up beside the lawman.

Pryor glanced at the man in annoyance. 'All right,' he said irritably, then looked again at Joel. 'Now...?'

The rider pushed ahead. 'Hell, he's been hit, Marshal. He's in no shape to talk.'

'If he can stand, he can talk,' Pryor said curtly.

'I don't know what's holding him up,' the man said, halted before Joel. 'Better let me take a look at that wound. You're bleeding bad.'

Joel stared. 'You a doctor?'

'Yep. Wingate's the name,' the physician said, and began to pull aside Kane's blood-soaked shirt.

Joel drew away. 'Forget me. I'm all right. Obliged if you'll see what you can do for my pa ... he's inside the house.'

Wingate said – 'In a minute.' – and, reaching into his brush coat pocket, produced a flat oilskin fold. Opening it, he obtained several pads of gauze, pressed them against Joel's wound.

'Hold that right there. I'll be back in a bit.'

Beckoning to several of the posse, he started for the house at a trot. Eli Pryor came off his horse stiffly, wearily. He pointed to the pistol in Joel's hand.

'Put that away ... your pa? ... you mean Amos Kane?'

Joel continued to hold the weapon. The marshal was still an unknown quantity as far as he was concerned. 'You were in the bank. You know that.'

'Heard you say it ... didn't mean it's true.'

Kane shook his head in disgust. 'Ask Pa ... if he's still alive.'

There was a rattle in the doorway of the

barn. The hostlers appeared, leading a team hitched to a light spring wagon. Kane waved them toward the house.

'Over there ... and get a mattress ... throw it in the back for him to lie on.'

Pryor waited until the wagon had passed. He pointed then at Berryman and Bill Taney. 'What about them?'

'Was either...?' A shiver raced through Joel, and his knees suddenly had no strength. He sat down slowly.

Pryor immediately took a half step forward, checked when the pistol in Joel's hand came up fast. 'I'm telling you again, put that iron away,' he ordered. 'Hell, man, I'm on your side. I've been trying to get something on Berryman for months.'

Joel studied the old lawman's seamy face in the growing daylight. Maybe – just maybe – Pryor was speaking the truth. 'Might have told me that sooner,' he said. 'Could have saved a lot of trouble ... and killing.'

'Told you? How the devil could I? Only saw you twice ... at the bank and here.'

'I was with Berryman and the others when you ran into us on the trail. Didn't you see...?'

'It was dark. I didn't see anybody plain except Cass Berryman. Why didn't you speak up?'

'That *vaquero* of Berryman's was holding a knife to Pa's throat. Would have killed him if I'd said anything.'

Pryor wagged his head helplessly. 'Lot more to this than I figured. You're going to have to answer some questions.'

'Only thing he's going to do right now,' Wingate said, coming from the house, 'is climb into that wagon. Got to get him to town so's I can dress that bullet hole properly.'

Joel looked anxiously at the doctor. 'Pa ... will he be all right?'

Wingate nodded. 'Sure. Be fine. Lost a bit of blood, but he's a tough old rooster. He'll make it.' The physician turned to the marshal. 'Eli, you want the straight of things around here, go see those two hostlers.

They're talking their heads off.'

Reaching down, the physician helped Joel to his feet, then motioned to one of the posse members and said: 'Let's get him in the wagon.'

They half carried, half walked him to the vehicle, placed him on the mattress beside Amos. The older Kane grinned at his son.

'Reckon we did it, eh?'

'We did. Doc says you'll be all right.'

'Sure. How about you? Looks like you've been bleeding like a stuck hog.'

Joel sighed. 'Felt worse ... and I've sure'n hell felt better a lot of times.'

'They told me Cass and Bill Taney are both dead. Was afraid when I saw you going through that door...'

'Be about enough of that jabbering,' Wingate broke in as he climbed onto the wagon seat and gathered up the reins. 'Don't want you two talking yourselves to death.'

Amos glanced at the medical man, grinned again at Joel. 'Ain't no danger, Doc,' he said. 'Us Kanes are mighty hard to kill.'

This Large Print Book, for people
who cannot read normal print,
is published under the auspices of
THE ULVERSCROFT FOUNDATION

... we hope you have enjoyed this book.
Please think for a moment about those
who have worse eyesight than you ...
and are unable to even read or enjoy
Large Print without great difficulty.

You can help them by sending a
donation, large or small, to:

**The Ulverscroft Foundation,
1, The Green, Bradgate Road,
Anstey, Leicestershire, LE7 7FU,
England.**
or request a copy of our brochure for
more details.

The Foundation will use all donations
to assist those people who are visually
impaired and need special attention
with medical research, diagnosis
and treatment.

Thank you very much for your help.